Buddha Boy

& The Witches in the Woods

Zalen Zed

Red Raptor Books

Contents

For my son, Brilliant, if he should ever doubt how much I love him, on the occasion of his twelfth birthday.

CHAPTER ONE

How my life turned upside down

I became rich when I was little because the only words my father spoke to my mother in between their days of silence were curses and I earnt 10p for each one.

She might be a waitress, he'd say, but she's still your mum.

It was lot of money back then because he didn't have what my mother called a proper job anymore. We lived in a council flat with low boxed rooms on the fourteenth floor of a housing estate with a lift that alternately smelt of pee or bleach, surrounded by graffiti in Bristol. He used to be an accountant but now he stayed at home, never went out, and wrote books which never sold.

He insisted she put the shopping receipts under his bedroom door which inevitably provoked arguments about why she had been frivolous in buying donuts of no nutritional value—or vitamins, which clearly had—for my four-year old sister and I, but still bought himself beer and cigarettes.

I kept my winnings in a secret place, the battery compartment of a toy robot on my shelf, to stop money disappearing.

My friends at Middlescotte Primary School were the only respite from the tension in the flat which added to the hurt I felt at the thought of leaving them, when my father arranged for me to sit the entrance exam for what he called Harry Potter boarding school, because he knew I loved Harry Potter.

He downloaded extra books and made me study every morning throughout the holidays, although I was allowed to play with my friends in the concrete play area outside, where a kid had once been stabbed, if my mother accompanied us.

He also gave me extra lessons in mathematics in the evening and taught me how to construct twenty-times tables which I had to memorise. I was permitted Brawl Stars for one hour in the evening as a treat.

He made me sit practice exams in English, Mathematics and Problem Solving under timed exam conditions and marked the papers with me, analysing the errors and suggesting strategies to overcome them, even in creative writing.

For example, every short story needed a beginning, middle and an end and have at least one twist at the end based on the title, as if he knew what made a good story in his books about how to quit drinking, which he never could.

He told me I only needed 90% to win a scholarship which was easy, he said, because I could still make 10% errors. No pressure(!)

I was embarrassed because I was the only child in a three-piece suit and tie at the interview and entrance test. All the other pupils wore school uniform but my father didn't think my Middlescotte sweatshirt was appropriate.

To be fair to him, he also wore a three-piece suit and tie when he took me, which I didn't even know he had, and shaved for the first time in as long as I can remember.

It was strange seeing him sitting on the train opposite me, all dressed up like an accountant when he usually pottered around our small flat in a T-shirt and pants with his hairy legs.

We got a taxi, another first, from the station down the long winding country lanes through the rolling green hills of the Mendips. My father didn't speak, nervously watching the meter rise.

We finally reached a high metal gate with a sign 'The Grange Grammar Boarding School' and the driver pressed the intercom buzzer, asked for my name, and then we drove under the old stone arch entrance down another winding lane to a castle-like fortress. Four-storey high Georgian pillars stood either side of the wide stone steps leading to giant double doors making me feel even smaller than I felt standing beside my father.

We stepped into a grand entrance hall onto chess patterned marble floors with wood-paneled walls and the School Coat of Arms, hanging between huge wooden boards with names and letters at the end inscribed in gold, BA, MA or Ph.D, Oxon.

It was more like a cold museum than a school, with no rainbows anywhere, nor any pupils' drawings on the walls, like at

Middlescotte. The beamed roof was high enough to house a T-Rex and made me feel even smaller.

They asked us to sit in a room with roll-back leather couches and high winged leather armchairs in front of a giant open lit coal fireplace burning with rising flames.

A lady arrived with a boy with a prefect badge on his lapel.

'I'm Miss Pearl, Sales and Marketing Manager, and this is Elvis, he'll be giving you a brief tour.'

We stood up and followed him back to reception and he stopped with his back to the crest between the honour's boards.

'This is our Coat of Arms, and the school motto reads, *Ex Spinis Uvas*, which means grapes from thorns. The pictures represent our school's values: the unicorn is a symbol of purity, innocence and power; the phoenix is a symbol of resurrection; The sword is a symbol of honour; and the scales, a symbol of justice. Follow me.'

We stepped out the high front door we'd just come in.

'This building dates back to the Middle-ages, it was founded in 1532 by Royal Charter, I'll show you where the school began, we call it the cornerstone because it was the first brick ever laid.'

He stopped by a bronze plaque at the bottom of a huge tower on the far right of the building, which was fenced off by a low thick corded rope.

'We're not supposed to step across it but I can never remember the inscription,' he stepped on the mud, '"Herein lies the cornerstone of our greatness for centuries to come. May it shed light on our darkness and be a tribute to the values we hold as firm." It's not the actual stone, though, that's buried in the foundations, obviously, and there are dungeons above that, and the textiles classrooms above that.'

'Dungeons?' I said, 'What are they like?'

'I don't know. I've never won the headmaster's award. That's the prize if you get enough house points for services to the community.'

I felt my father nudge me on the shoulder. 'You can do that,' he said.

'I'm not going to lie, it's practically impossible. Only one student in the whole school is awarded it every year, but I suppose that makes it more special.'

'Alex is very special,' he said, embarrassing me.

'Follow me. There are four hundred rooms in the building, including the new dorms, and the site is ten acres, including all the sports fields, horse riding fields and we've got our own farm. But I think it's going to close because the foxes keep stealing the lambs and piglets.'

I thought that was sad.

When we returned, I was relieved to sit down, but not for long.

Miss Pearl offered my father a cup of tea, which he was profusely grateful like tickets for the FA Cup, while I was taken alone for the test.

The test was easy, and I finished before everyone else but still went back through every answer like my father had told me. And then I had an interview with the headmaster.

On the way home my father made me repeat it verbatim, evaluating every answer as if there were a prize at the end. He told me, again, it wasn't important what I said but the way I said them, considering the pros and cons of each question, like exams are necessary for success in life, but stressful, even though the interview was over.

When the Bursar made a visit a few weeks later, I have never seen our flat so clean, my father had glued the peeling wall paper in the corner, and the bible and Oxford English Dictionary strategically placed on the mantlepiece above the electric fire.

My father and I were all dressed-up in our three-piece suits again.

I wanted to know my results but the Bursar said they didn't give them which I thought was unfair.

I had almost forgotten about the Grange when months later my father proudly showed me the acceptance letter announcing I had won a full scholarship.

I tried to smile because he was so happy but I couldn't help thinking about my friends going to Fishdown Comprehensive, just around the corner, and didn't understand why I had to be different.

My father insisted it was still my choice but I didn't buy that.

He seemed to enjoy repeating it was just like Harry Potter's school, but I didn't buy that either.

To me, it was the dinosaur place and the thought of living there was beyond scary to imagine, so I tried not to think about it all summer except when commiserating with friends in the concrete playing area outside—they all thought my father was cruel—until the unavoidable day came when my mother tearfully packed my suitcase and prepared my second-hand blazer, with the school coat of arms on the top pocket, and charcoal grey trousers for the morning.

My mother didn't want me to leave.

I tried to be strong but I cried too, right in front of the Grand Entrance, when they waved goodbye in the taxi and left me outside.

I was on my own at twelve.

The House Matron rallied a prefect to carry my luggage to her dorm office and consulted her computer.

'You have three options,' she said, 'I can put you in with Charles, he knows the ropes, been with us since kindergarten, very sporty, bold and brash, loves getting stuck in at his Rugby.

'Or there's Arthur, joined us after Prep School in London, very outgoing, never stuck for words and very funny, you'd like him—everyone does—fine actor,' she smiled.

'Or,' she hesitated with a curious frown, as if in two minds whether or not to make the suggestion, 'there's still Mason, *again*. Let's just say he's a bit different. Quiet, self-absorbed, not strange, a little reserved, perhaps, but an incredibly bright little Indian boy. Into D&D. Hard to know what he's thinking or feeling sometimes. Not like an alien or anything ...'

'Mason,' I said, without hesitation.

'Are you sure? He's only been here a year, parents off yachting around the world, whereas William, you know, knows the place like the back of his hand, probably better than I do. And I don't really know Mason, nobody does. He doesn't share an awful lot and you might feel a bit distant.

'Or Arthur, yes Arthur, the more I think about it, you'd really like him. He'd bring you out of your shell in no time at all. Shall we say Arthur, then? He's very charming. All the teachers love him.'

'I'd prefer Mason, Miss.' I lied, 'I love D&D'. I didn't like the idea of sharing with a rugby jock or actor wanting to be centre of attention.

'Now do you? Isn't that a coincidence, so does Mason. Perhaps I'm wrong after all,' she crinkled her nose, 'are you sure? Then I don't see why not, the company will be good for him. Right then,' she tapped on her keyboard, 'Mason and Alex it is. Room 87. I'll get one of the prefects to take you and your luggage there. And come to see how you're settling in later.'

When she told the prefect outside which room to take my luggage to, he raised his eyebrows but didn't say a word until we were out of earshot.

'What's wrong with Room 87?' I asked him.

'It's not the room, it's who's in it,' he grimaced. 'It doesn't matter, you'll find out soon enough. But don't say I didn't warn you. Do a term and ask for a transfer, trust me, they'll understand. You won't be the first. I think you're the third who's tried.'

'What's so bad about Mason, is he mean?'

The prefect looked up and to the right as if he hadn't considered that, stopping in the long corridor and putting my suitcase down for a rest. 'Not like that. I don't think anybody really knows what he is. It's like cracking the enigma code. His parents probably don't even know what he thinks. He's like a secret within a secret within a secret, but you judge for yourself. That's what we're here for. To make our own decisions.' He carried on to room 87 and was about to knock on the door when it opened itself.

'Good luck, Alex' the prefect shook my hand and quickly walked away.

I took a deep breath and entered the room which was as big as our living-room, but without peeling wallpaper, and appeared empty except for a shelving cabinet stacked full of books until the door closed behind me and I turned round to see a skinny dark-skinned fragile boy with glasses which had a blue patch over the right lens with a picture of Sonic the hedgehog.

'You must be Alex. I like you.'

'You must be Mason. But how do you know my name?'

He shrugged. 'The same way I knew there was someone at the door. Be still and listen. This is your area, cupboard, desk and bed. This is my area.' He indicated his and the book case.

'First rule, nothing, and I mean nothing, leaves this room except the spiritual. All warfare is based on deception. 'Appear weak when you are strong, and strong when you are weak'—Sun Tzu, The Art of War. I have already said too much.

'Second rule, no distractions. No music without headphones, no farting, humming, whistling or chewing gum and no interruptions when I'm meditating. My mind needs peace to escape.

'Third rule, don't break the first two; the last three people to break them are no longer here for a reason.'

'No farting?'

He looked over his glasses at me with his one eye, 'do I look like I'm joking?' He offered his hand, 'Mason Armitage. Pleased to meet you.'

After which, without another word, he turned and assumed the full lotus position on his bed, neck perfectly straight, chin level, the back of his open hands on his knees, and closed his eye.

I tried to unpack as quietly as possible, in between looking back at him sitting there motionlessly, like trying to catch someone out in a game of statues, but the only thing that moved was his chest gently rising and falling with each breath. I have never seen a kid be so perfectly still before.

After unpacking, I opened my eReader with all the books my father had downloaded for me.

I thought I read a lot, but I looked over at his book case and it was like I had barely started. There weren't the usual Percy Jackson, Harry Potter and Beast Quest series, which I thought everyone my age read, but strange titles like The Catcher in the Rye, The Finger of the Gods, The Dead Sea Scrolls and The Buddhist Bible. It was like he had taken a different path to most kids which made me think, a) that might explain why people didn't seem to like him, and, b) why he didn't seem to like them much either.

I sensed he was aware of a whole different world than I had ever experienced.

Imagine, I thought, if I'm sharing with some kind of enlightened being or reincarnated Dalai Lama?

I determined to undertake careful observation of him, and track his comings and goings in my journal because who knew how long the opportunity would last and it would be a distraction from the homesickness I already felt.

I also had a feeling I might learn a bit about myself in the process.

He still hadn't moved when I returned to my book.

And then he farted without breaking his serene smile.

Chapter Two

I just want to go home

The first few weeks would have been hell, were it not for Mason.

It wasn't the days. We were kept so busy from wake-up call, shower and matins through classes that changed room every hour, in everything from Algebra to Latin, there was barely time to pee.

It was the nights when I missed home so much it hurt like a heartsectomy.

I tried to put on a brave front but one night after lights out it was too much.

I rolled up in the foetal position under the duvet not to be heard because I couldn't stop myself crying, like an illness that had taken over my entire body.

The first time Mason didn't say anything, but a few nights later, the third time, he turned his torch on.

I thought he was going to be angry and tell me I'd broken the second rule or call the House Matron and I'd get in trouble.

'You need to call home.'

'I ca ... ca ... can't.' I sobbed. He knew we were not allowed phones for the first term.

He jumped out of bed, turned his laptop on and grabbed his headset.

'Drastic times call for drastic measures. What's their number?'

'I ... I ... I don't know. It's in my phone.' I heaved like it was an impossible situation without any solution.

'No problem.' I heard him tapping on the keyboard, 'come here, is that it?'

I climbed out of bed and there on the screen was a window labelled Teacher Portal with a picture of me, my attendance, my grades, medical history, my address and my mother's and father's mobile numbers.

'Mother or father?' He asked.

The shock alleviated my tears and I suddenly had to think and checked my watch, 'But it's nine thirty?'

'That'll be early for them. Which?'

'My mother. But how?'

He tapped on the keyboard, opened Skype in a small window, copy and pasted the number, pressed call and handed me the headset.

I heard the phone ringing and my heart swelled at the thought it was my mother's phone ringing, and then I heard her voice, 'Hello?'

'Mama...' I immediately burst into tears again.

'Alex, Alex ...? Is that you?'

I sniffed. 'Yes, mama ... I want to come home.'

'Of course, my darling. We miss you so much ... It's Alex, he wants to come home.'

'I want to go to Fishdown with my friends,' I snivelled, 'I promise I'll work hard.'

'Of course, darling—let go of my phone, he's being bullied, I told you it was a bad idea—Don't worry, my darling boy, we'll come and collect you tomorrow. I said let go...'

'Alex?' It was my father. I expected the worst. 'Can you hear me?'

'Yes, papa.' I snorted trying to hide my crying.

'Do you have permission to make this call?'

I looked at Mason vigorously shaking his head, 'No, papa.'

Mason put his head in his hands.

'Are you being bullied?'

'No, papa.'

'He's not being bullied. You're being ridiculous. Have you had an accident?

'No, papa, I'm fine.'

'Listen,' he softened, 'I know it's not easy but you have to be strong, Alex. It's hard to understand now, but this is your future at stake. You don't want to end up like me, powerless. You have to be the boss—he's not coming home, get away from me—it's only a few more weeks and it'll be half-term. We all miss you, but we can handle a few more weeks, right?'

'Yes, papa.'

'Fine, have the phone then.'

'Alex, this is your mother. Ignore him, he's drunk. I'm coming to collect you right now.'

'DON'T TELL HIM I'M DRUNK!'

I started crying again. 'I'm fine, mama, honestly.'

'Are you sure? I mean it, I will get on the bus right now.'

'I know, mama. I love you. I said I'm fine,' tears rolled down my cheek, 'I better go.'

She told me to sleep on it and if I still felt the same way in the morning, she didn't care what anyone said, she was coming to collect me.

They started arguing again as she wished me goodnight and sweet dreams and, for a moment, it was just like being back home and I could picture the Bible and Oxford English Dictionary still sitting on the mantlepiece above the electric fire.

I heaved a few deep breaths, took off the headset and handed it back to Mason.

'Are they always like that?' I didn't realise he was still sitting right next to me and heard everything. I nodded and I don't know why, but I laughed, 'Yeah.'

'Do you feel better?' He put his hand on my shoulder.

'How did you do that?'

'You have to find the weakest link in the system. Who are the smartest and most trustworthy people in the school?

'The teachers?'

'Who is the weakest link in the teachers?'

'Who is the worst teacher?'

'You're forgetting the objective. Who is the most forgetful teacher in the school—Miss Hardy, History, of course. What does she do every lesson registration before she logs in?'

'Wish us good morning?'

'Almost. Open her hard-backed green notebook. Why?'

'She can't remember the login?'

'Correct! And where does she look exactly in her little green notebook? On the last page. And what happens when she forgets her little green notebook and can't leave the class unsupervised? She sends a pupil volunteer to get it. And who volunteers out of the kindness of his heart? And I know exactly where to look and it's even labelled 'Teacher Portal login'. Username: phardy' and password: 'Hilaryclinton', capital H, one word. I even learnt her politics for free.'

'You're a genius.'

'It's child's play. But if you're ever short an A.'

'Won't she find out?'

'You're right. Access Records. But why would she go through her access records for no reason? She's entering grades on it every night. Do you think she's going to know the reason for every occasion she logged in—it's just one time and date stamp among probably thousands—especially someone that forgetful.'

'What about my father? What if he calls the school?'

'And get you expelled? Does he want that? Of course not, by the sounds of it. Remember, all warfare is based on deception. Appear weak when you are strong, and strong when you are weak.'

That is Mason all over. And I wouldn't want him any other way, no matter what anybody else says.

We were now in this together, and I'd die for him.

CHAPTER THREE

The missing boy

It was so cold on the Rugby field Mr Swanson was wearing a woolly hat, his tracksuit and gloves whereas we had to wear our T-shirts and shorts shivering in the line-up. I felt sorry for Mason because he was always the last to be picked.

During the match Charlie Montague-the boy miss had originally suggested sharing with—and twice the size of anyone else in the year, made a ferocious tackle landing his full weight on Mason's ankle *after* he'd just passed the ball. Charlie didn't apologise and even objected to the foul being called by the whistle.

Mason had to be carried off, but I had Montague in my sights now, however big he was. The taller they are, the harder they fall, my father always said. I was like a hawk waiting for my opportunity to pounce and when Mr Swanson wasn't looking and Charlie had the ball, turned and slammed my boot behind his knee and he went down like a sack of potatoes, face first into the mud.

He jumped up and pushed me by the shoulders with such force I went flying back and landed on my bottom but I got up and charged into him head first, like running into a truck.

He swung with his right fist and caught me on jaw, but I got up again as the crowd built around us and started chanting, 'fight, fight, fight, fight'.

I couldn't reach his head and punched his body with flailing fists. But he swung a left uppercut catching me on the chin and I was down again with a bloodied lip.

I tasted the bitter blood on my tongue and Charlie raised his hands in victory, but I staggered to my feet and was about to go for him again when Swanson suddenly pushed his way through the crowd and grabbed us both by the collar and marched us off the field.

I was hyperventilating and still wanting to fight, while Mr Swanson gave us a lecture on winning the fight on the field by the rules of the game.

I was certain I was going to be expelled, but Mr Swanson made us apologise and shake hands 'like gentlemen', which I grudgingly conceded to.

Mr Swanson sent Montague back on the field and felt my jaw with both hands and asked me to turn my head from side to side before saying nothing was broken, just swollen, and made me repeat it was just a normal rugby accident before sending me to the sickbay.

Which is how I ended up sitting beside Mason in a wheelchair with an icepack around his ankle while we waited for the doctor.

Two policemen passed the open door and for a moment I thought they were looking for me and then told Mason what happened.

'I know why,' Mason said, 'but you shouldn't have done that.'

'You didn't even have the ball,' I objected.

'Not what you did, but *how* you did it. What were you trying to achieve?'

'I wanted to hurt him, of course.'

'Do you really think you're going to hurt him where he's strongest? Having a fist fight with a knucklehead like Montague is like giving him cheesecake. He relishes it and he's rather good at it.' He nodded at his ankle and smiled. 'You should have looked for his Achilles heel.'

'Sprain his ankle?' I asked perplexed.

'Not literally. Think about what would *really* hurt him.' He tapped his head. 'Think. Don't signpost it for the whole world to see. Think about where he's most vulnerable.'

'I know that. I went for the back of his knee.'

He shook his head sadly. 'That's physical.' He tapped his head again. 'Up here. Think. I've said too much already. You can work the rest out for yourself.'

The doctor arrived and confirmed that Mason's ankle and my jaw weren't broken but we still needed to go to the hospital for X-rays, just in case, and the House matron took us in her car.

Hours of waiting later the doctor's diagnosis was proved correct; Mason just had a sprained ankle, and was given a large foam boot tied with Velcro straps and crutches, and I was told to keep an icepack on my jaw, which was a bit ironic considering it was still freezing when we got outside late in the evening.

In the car on the way back, the House Matron told us she would have to let our parents know we'd had a rugby accident but we were OK. I looked at Mason with relief in my eyes on the backseat behind her.

'Thank you, miss,' Mason nodded at me.

'Yes, thank you, miss,' I said.

'If it's not one thing, it's another,' she said, 'I haven't stopped all day. I thought it was enough dealing with the Police all morning before you two showed up and bang—there goes my Saturday night. But I'm not complaining.'

'No, of course not,' Mason said, 'it's very kind of you to go the extra mile for us. We're very grateful. We saw the police leaving.'

I raised my eyebrows at Mason, and behind the seat he held his flat hand out like a stop sign to be still and wait.

After a long pause she said, 'I suppose you're going to find out anyway,' Mason smiled at me like his tactic had worked, 'the Police are going to make an announcement on TV tonight. This is all I need this Michaelmas: One of our pupils has gone missing.'

I saw Mason's eye light up accentuated by his thick lenses with all his attention suddenly intent on her rear-view mirror, 'a runaway?'

'That's what we thought, but we've obviously searched all the grounds with the Police using sniffer dogs, who ended up running in circles around the rugby field. A local volunteer village team has been traipsing through the fields and undergrowth all day and found nothing. His poor father is distraught. It's his only child.

Money means nothing to him. I suppose you can't put a price on your child, but fifty thousand pounds for any information leading to his whereabouts is beyond most people's salary—certainly my teacher's salary. I hope it isn't too late.'

'How very sad,' Mason said. 'I hope it's not my friend.'

'He's in your year. Do you know Patrick Mackensie?'

'Oh no, not Patrick.'

'I thought you didn't have any friends, Mason?'

'Yes he does,' I said, 'me.'

'It must be all that D&D you play together.'

'Do you play D&D?' Mason whispered to me, and I rolled my eyes and nodded silently at the back of her head. 'Oh, yes, we both love D&D. And so does Patrick,' he winked at me, which looked funny beside Sonic the hedgehog smiling from his eyepatch, 'when did he go missing?'

'We don't really know exactly. The last time I saw him was lights out two days ago and nobody can remember seeing him in the morning or at breakfast and he was absent for morning registration.

'We obviously checked all the CCTV outside the building but there's not a trace. He just vanished like a ghost in the night.' The electronic gate opened and we pulled in through the high arched entrance and I noticed the light on in the little hut behind the high wall.

'We have 24-hour security and they saw nothing.'

'Did they interview his roommate?' I asked.

'I thought you said he was your friend. He didn't have a roommate.'

'Forensics obviously checked his room,' Mason said quickly.

'Nobody else's fingerprints, no forced entry, all his school equipment, personal possessions and every item of his wardrobe is accounted for, even his pyjamas, nothing is missing. He just seems to have spirited away.'

She parked in front of our House wing around the side of the giant building and she undid her seatbelt.

'Please don't worry the others. Nothing has ever happened like this before. I'll just get the chair.'

She returned pushing the wheelchair and opened the rear door and Mason carefully swung his bandaged foot out and she helped him lift him to his feet and into the chair and I passed him his crutches which he rested across on the arms of the chair.

She gave us special permission to use the staff lift while he was incapacitated, which included me as his assigned helper, which was pretty cool, and passes for us to leave class at any time for toilet or early lunch.

We could basically come and go as we pleased, no questions asked, and obviously excused from Games for the rest of term, and able to study in our room or the library.

In fact, you couldn't wish for a more convenient set of circumstances to have the time and convenience to investigate the mysterious disappearance of a missing person, which I already suspected Mason was biting at the bit to begin.

Like Watson, I had every intention to record the events of Mason-Sherlock Holmes-Armitage in my journal, because I didn't have a clue where to begin.

But I'd bet fifty thousand pounds he did.

CHAPTER FOUR

The moody blues

I t's a good thing I'm not a betting man because Mason is as unpredictable as the weather.

Where it came from, I have no idea, but the next day he was unbearably miserable and antagonistic. When you're sharing a room with someone, you can't get away from it.

Overnight he was no longer awake meditating on his bed when I woke up but huddled under his duvet and refused to get dressed or go to class. I suppose he couldn't exactly do the full lotus with his sprained ankle but surely that didn't stop him getting dressed.

The doctor came to the room and gave him painkillers and a seven-day sick note for rest and recuperation, and I told him I'd get copies of any classwork and share all my notes, but there was no gratitude.

He was even rude to the House Matron when she visited and point blank refused to talk beyond yes and no answers.

She told me outside she had warned me that he got like this sometimes and not to take it personally and that it would pass.

But as the days passed, he showed no signs of improvement and after his third outburst I decided if he couldn't sort himself out, I needed to confront him.

'You don't understand, I'm a cripple, an outcast.' He said vehemently. 'That's what they call people in my country who can't sit. I'm worthless, nothing, a vile pig. Don't soil your soul with me. I don't want your pity. Leave me to my darkness. Just leave me alone, please?'

'No. I'm not letting you carry on like this. It's gone too far.'

'Why are you torturing me? Can't you see I'm in pain?' He was almost in tears, pleading with me, 'please, please, please just leave me alone. I don't want to be here. I've had enough. Can't you see that? I've sprained my ankle!'

'No. You haven't sprained your ankle. You've sprained your spirit. And my dad may be a useless broke chain-smoking drunk writer, or worse, but he never stopped trying to do what he believes in. 'I don't care if I lost the fight against Montague, but I never stayed down, I forced myself to get up. And now it's your turn to force yourself to get up and fight whatever's going on in your head.'

I sat on the edge of his bed, 'remember when I just started and you told me I needed to call home because I was homesick.' I felt my eyes feeling watery, but forced myself to continue, 'that was like an angel of kindness, and you can curse me as long as I live, but I will never forget that. It is who you are. It's beneath all the learning in books and philosophy, which I can't hope to ever understand like you, but I know it's a glow of loving-kindness, and if you've got that, nobody or nothing can take it away from you.'

He pulled the duvet over his head and started to cry, 'I'm sorry, I'm sorry, I just can't handle this. Please just go away.'

'You're wrong. You can. I'm not going to let you stop anymore. I'm warning you, I'm an immovable mountain. You need to call home.'

'What?' He suddenly flung the duvet back, 'are you out of your mind? Have you any idea what my step-father will do to me? I'll be a family disgrace. They'll disown me. Abandon me. Cut me off from my inheritance. You're crazier than me. I'll be on the streets.'

'You already are.' I logged into the Teacher Portal using the username and password he had given me and searched for his details. There was his picture and there was his mother's and step-father's long mobile numbers.

'Mother or step-father?'

'I'm not telling you.'

'Step-father it is.' I opened the skype application and copy and pasted the number into it. He tried to scramble out of bed but he was too slow with his ankle. 'It's ringing. Do you want me to start or … Hello, is this Mr Armitage? Can you accept a call from your son, Mason, please?'

Mason looked up at the ceiling as if the sky had just collapsed.

'Who are you?' The voice said.

'My name's Alex, and you don't know me, but Mason is my best friend and he's not very well. Would you like to talk to him?' I took off the headset and held it out to him.

Mason reluctantly took it. 'Hello father?' And as soon as he heard the voice on the other end he started crying again.

I quietly left the room.

Sometimes you can't take no for an answer.

CHAPTER FIVE

5 ways to find a missing boy

I'm not a psychologist so I don't know whether Mason was meditating to gain insight, like he claimed, or to avoid some kind of crippling depression, but the next day I was so relieved, and quite amused, to see him sitting on the edge of his bed meditating in the half-leg lotus position, with his other leg flat on the floor, and the same serene smile.

When he finally opened his eyes, I could see the old Mason was back.

'About the other night,' he said, 'I think I owe you an apology. I suspect a cosmic field distorted ...'

'What other night? I'm sorry but I haven't a clue what you are referring to.'

Mason bummed his lips, dropped his eyes and then looked back up, 'thank you, Alex. I mean that.' He paused respectfully before excitedly continuing, 'Now about the case. There isn't much time and a boy's life I sincerely suspect may be in our hands while we speak.'

If I had been a betting man, I would have just won fifty thousand pounds; I knew he'd have a plan and I had my figurative pen at the ready.

'You will be my legs and ears. I'm damned if I can get anywhere much around on these. But it is imperative that you follow my instructions to the letter. It's quite clear to me now where everybody, including the Police, have gone wrong. They are looking for the physical Patrick, whereas they should be looking for the *spiritual* Patrick. I can't explain it all now, but it came to me in my meditation like a lucid dream. Don't look at me like I'm crazy, OK, I was crazy, but I'm not now.'

'So where is he?'

'Right here. He never left.'

'Are you talking spiritually or physically? I'm sorry, I'm a bit confused to be honest.'

'Both.'

I took a deep breath. 'Are you sure you're feeling alright?'

'Never been better. Try and think about it like this. If all the evidence points to the fact that he never left, like Sherlock Holmes said, 'when you have eliminated the impossible, whatever remains, however improbable, must be the truth.'

'I think that makes sense. So where exactly is he? There are four hundred rooms, and Elvis said this site is 10 acres.'

'Haven't the foggiest. But that's not the priority right now.'

'I thought we were supposed to find him.'

'Yes, spiritually before physically, like I just said, which is where you come in, doctor.'

'Doctor?'

'Doctor Watson, get it? But I'm sure you will be one day, a psychologist I suspect, you just don't know it yet, but you're very good you know. I learnt more in five minutes with you than five years with counsellors. Loving-kindness, it says it all really.'

'You used to go to a counsellor?'

'We're getting off topic and we haven't time for this.'

'Since you were six?'

'Believe me, if I could run, I'd be out of that door in a shot. We need to get inside the mind of Patrick Mackensie. Inside his soul. Inside his very spirit. Think of it like we're starting from ground zero and need to rebuild those giant twin towers that have just disappeared into thin air but all the other particles around have a memory of it. Matter and anti-matter. The physicality is just an illusion.'

'You have totally lost me now.'

'It doesn't matter—forgive the pun—we need to find out everything we can about Patrick Mackensie's hopes, dreams and ambitions before anyone else can, without showing any interest at all.' Before I could ask how, he continued. 'Starting with his room. You need to sneak in there without being seen while everyone else is doing Games next period.'

'Uh-uh, no way am I doing that alone. And it's bound to be locked.'

'Fine, you can push me. The House Matron will have the key.'

'There is no way she is just going to give you the key.'

'Leave her to me. Second, we need to speak to all his friends, they might tell us things they wouldn't have told the Police. Third, teachers. I can get his grades online, but what did they know about his hopes, dreams and ambitions. What clubs, societies, competitions did he enter. Fourth, social media. I bet his whole world is online, everyone else's is. Fifth, family. The step-father. Get him on the phone, record the call on Skype. I'm an old friend and I miss him and want to know if I can do anything to help. Was there a family crisis? You'd be good at that.'

'And then what?'

'I meditate. The answer will just come to me.'

'That's not much like Sherlock Holmes.'

'Sherlock Holmes didn't have Buddhism. Believe me, if Sherlock Holmes had Buddhism he wouldn't have been defeated by Moriarty. He would have seen that coming. What are you waiting for? Help me into the chair. We've got to see his room. His life, wherever he is, may depend on it.'

CHAPTER SIX

The crime scene

Mason knocked on the House Matron's door and I pushed him in when she answered.

'Mason? How nice of you to visit. How are you feeling today?'

'Much better, thank you, miss. I wanted to apologise to you for the way I behaved the other day. I'm sorry I didn't feel like talking.'

'That's quite alright. What can I do for you today? I should be having lunch but I'm in the middle of organising the Parent Teacher Evening. Let's book a time to talk properly if you'd like to? How about Period 5?'

'That's very kind of you, Miss. Can I get back to you on that but I could do with your help on another matter. You know Patrick and I liked to play D&D.'

'Yes, I think you mentioned that.'

'Alex and I ...'

'I know Alex loves D&D, you don't need my permission to play, as long as it's in your free time. Was there anything else?'

'Thank you, miss. It's just that Patrick borrowed my D&D book and we can't play without it.'

'Can't you get one from the library?'

'They don't have any D&D books, and it's hard because I can't do any sports in my free time and I'm so bored. Alex said he'll play with me if I could just have my book back. But I don't want to cause a fuss if it's too much trouble.'

She checked her watch and sighed. 'I'm sorry Mason, I simply haven't got time to go all the way to the sixth floor right now for a D&D book. The things I get asked never cease to amaze me.'

'You don't have to. Alex can take me, and we'll bring the key straight back, I promise. Please, miss?'

'I really shouldn't, but it's just one D&D book, is that right? The Police have already been in so I suppose it can't do any harm.' She put a plastic card into the machine by her computer and then handed it to us, 'Room 78 but don't touch anything else, it's still technically a crime scene, and bring this straight back to me, is that clear?'

'Thank you so much, miss,' he took the key card, 'you're very kind.'

'I'm not paid enough for this. Now you've got your D&D book, was there anything else, because I really need to finish this PTA rota?'

We shook our heads smiling from ear to ear and left.

Outside the door Mason twirled the card key like a prize.

'I told you,' he winked, 'child's play.'

We took the staff lift to the sixth floor of the accommodation wing and I pushed Mason's wheelchair down the long silent dormitory floor corridor to room 78.

Mason looked over his shoulders both ways before he put the key card in the slot on the wall beside the handle and the little light below blinked green and I opened the door.

I felt like I was stepping into a dead man's cave, although I didn't know whether he was dead or still alive, and held the door open so Mason could wheel himself in.

The room's layout was a mirror image of ours, they must all be identical I thought, but the décor couldn't have been more different. There was a large red poster of a lonely sad puppy facing the camera with the slogan, '8 out of 10 Dogs Don't cope when left alone' with the RSPCA logo in the corner, surrounded by sketches of lambs, chickens, and piglets above his desk.

'He loves animals,' I said.

A pirate's scarf was wrapped over the top of the lampshade on the desk. The drawings and sketch pads and coloured pencils, were all neatly lined up, someone had clearly tidied up. I went to open the desk drawer and Mason suddenly shrieked, 'Stop!' I turned to look at him for an explanation and he held his hands up, 'fingerprints!'

'I'm just looking for your D&D book,' I smiled.

And he shrugged, 'fair enough.'

I opened the drawer and there were a few Marvel comics, nothing out of the ordinary, 'Immortal X-men', 'Miracleman: The

Silver Age' and 'Savage Avengers', and a few loose Maltesers. 'He likes Maltesers.' I couldn't resist taking one and ate it.

'That's disgusting,' he said, 'you don't know how long it's been sitting in that drawer.'

'They're delicious,' I took another one, 'Maltesers are my mother's Christmas treat.'

'I can't stand them; they remind too much of counselling. Miss Proctor keeps a box of them in her metal filing cabinet for when we finish.'

'It's the only time my father allows chocolate in the house.' I finished the last one, and opened the large metal drawer below hoping to find more but there were only empty Malteser packets.

'Why would someone leave a drawer empty,' I asked Mason, 'I never have enough room to put anything. Didn't she say every item was accounted for and nothing was missing?'

Mason opened the cupboard. 'All his clothes seem to be there like she said; his school uniform, jeans, tracksuit, his sports gear' he opened the cupboard drawer, 'cricket box, shin pads, his fishing rod, a slingshot, a balaclava, his T-shirts, his pants, his socks'—his parents haven't collected anything –even his school shoes and three pairs of trainers.'

'Three?' I was shocked because I only had one pair, 'he must be rich.'

'His father owns a Chocolate factory,' Mason said, 'he should have been called Charlie!'

I laughed. 'But who would leave naked?' I shivered at the thought, 'unless he was taken against his will?' I frowned at Mason, 'I don't like this room. It gives me the creeps.'

'You're right. We're doing this all wrong, like the police. The empty drawer, that's it. Don't look for what he's got, his strengths, look for what he hasn't got, his weaknesses. Where he's vulnerable. What *can't* we see, that any normal kid would have, doctor?'

It seemed to give him a kick calling me that, so I let it slide, and part of me, I have to admit, was flattered, although unlike him, I doubted I was smart enough to ever be a real one.

'There are no pictures of his family?'

'Good,' he said scanning the book case, 'all his school textbooks are here, but wait, he hasn't got a Latin dictionary.'

'He probably uses the class ones.'

'But how does he do his homework?'

'In the library or google, that's easy.'

'But it's on the required texts list. The police wouldn't know that.'

'His school laptop should obviously be on his desk, unless the police took it, or in his bag? Where is his school bag?'

'Why would he take his Latin dictionary in his school bag?' Mason said, 'he was hardly planning on doing homework.'

'Don't you see?' I said, 'it's the most important think we have, all our stuff is in it.' I checked under the desk, inside and behind the cupboard, under the bed, but there was no bag. 'It must be in his locker,' I said.

'And if it isn't, it must be somewhere else.'

'But surely the police ...'

'Do you think they remember what it's like to be a kid after so many years? I don't think so. They have no idea how important a school bag is, but it's obvious to any kid. This is our greatest strength, Doctor. We're *just* kids, and nobody will be expecting us to investigate, or more importantly, save his life and win fifty-thousand pounds. We need to find that bag. But we've got to give the card key back or she might get suspicious.'

I took one last look back at the room as Mason wheeled himself out, like the last ever look Patrick Mackensie must have once taken himself before saying goodbye, wherever he was now, and closed the door.

CHAPTER SEVEN

The locker surprise

M ason knocked on the House Matron's door.

'Come in, oh it's you two. I'd forgotten all about you. You're lucky to catch me, I'm starving. I was just about to get something to eat. Did you find your D&D book?'

'No, miss,' Mason said sadly, returning the key card, 'it was a Christmas present from my father. Patrick promised he would give it back to me.'

'I'm so sorry. It clearly means a lot to you.'

Never mind Arthur, the drama scholar I was supposed to share with, Mason was such a good actor, and looked so forlorn I almost believed it really was a present from his father and Patrick had borrowed it.

'I wonder if we can look into getting you one from the student fund? I'm not promising or anything but email me the title and ISBN and I'll see what I can do. How about that?'

'That's very kind of you, miss, but,' he shrugged, 'it's OK, it won't be the same. It had an inscription to me, so it's kind of got sentimental value to me when I feel homesick.'

Give the guy an Oscar, I thought, the House Matron was the one looking forlorn now.

'I don't suppose you could check whether it was on the list of the items the Police confiscated?'

'Of course I can, I don't think there was much and I don't remember any books.' She tapped into her keyboard. 'Here we are. Let me see, yes, just laptop and phone. I'm sorry, Mason.'

'No school bag? That's where he usually kept it.'

'No, that must still be in his room.'

'It isn't, we checked,' I said.

'It must be in his locker,' Mason said.

She looked at her watch and sighed. 'I'm sorry Mason, I just don't have the time with the best will in the world to be running around all day looking for your D&D book.'

'I don't mind going with him,' I said.

'Fine,' she huffed, 'but this is the last time,' she tapped on her keyboard, and took out a key from her desk drawer. 'If it's not there, you will just have to live without it or order a new one. Don't lose this, it is a master key. Locker D19. Now I must eat. Scat. Be gone. Away.'

We grinned like a couple of hyenas and both said simultaneously, 'Thank you, miss.'

We made our way through the crowds of pupils returning from the canteen, like the sea parting before us, to Patrick's form room where his locker was.

There were the lockers lined against the wall and there was D19, the top red locker nearest the door, but a few pupils sitting on desks turned to look at us in the doorway, the wheelchair was conspicuous, and Mason backed himself out.

'It's too risky. They're going to wonder why we're looking in his locker.'

'Never mind taking his bag,' I said.

It was so frustrating because I could almost touch the red Locker from where I'd been standing and the thought of all the possible clues inside the bag.

'Go back in and look at the room timetable on the wall and tell me when it's free.'

When we returned to the room it was thankfully empty and Mason gave me a thumbs-up and quickly wheeled himself to the locker and handed me the key.

'Quick, someone could come in at any moment. Pass me the bag and I'll sit on. Why are you playing around—open the locker.'

'It won't open. It's jammed or something.'

'Alex. Stop. Take a deep breath. It's not like a normal key, it's a master key. Try again, gently.'

'I'm trying. It won't ... I did it.' And my relief at the door swinging open was suddenly replaced by horror, 'it's empty—just a scrunched-up packet of Maltesers!' I lifted out the packet with two fingers like a dirty rat.

'I knew it!' Mason clapped excitedly, which was the last thing I expected.

'The police must have taken it.' I examined the packet and it was half-full. 'Do you want one?'

'It's not on their list. No thanks, you might catch something.'

'Just one.' And carefully placed it on my tongue and munched. It was delicious. And I immediately had another.

'I made sure to check because I knew it wouldn't be.'

'Am I missing something?' I said with my mouth full of chocolate, 'if it's not in his room and it's not in his locker, where is it?'

'He's got it. This wasn't a kidnapping, it was planned. And, my friend, he planned it all. Careful you don't choke on them.'

'They're very addictive—Lunch!'

'It makes perfect sense now. Don't you see? He didn't pack his suitcase and hop on a bus, he wanted to travel light which means not very far, at least until he had the resources to provide for his needs. You can't fit much in a school bag, but it had to be just enough.'

'You can tell all that from an absent school bag?' I said my tongue twisting on yet another one and it reminded me of the taste of Christmas.

'Maybe he just lost his school bag,' I said.

Mason looked over the rim at his spectacles at me as if to say, really?

'OK,' I shrugged, 'he's got his school bag.'

'Thank you. Not many naked ghosts vanish into thin air carrying their school bag.'

'So where is he?'

'Teachers.'

'Excuse me?'

'I told you, room, teachers, friends, family. We need to interview his teachers.'

'You're going to interview his teachers?' I laughed. 'This, I've got to see.'

'Good. Because you're doing it.'

'Wait a second.'

'You have to, I'm not going to any lessons and it would look too obvious.'

'No, this!' I pulled out a memory stick from the bag of Maltesers.

'O.M.G.' Mason mouthed.

'I'm a genius,' I popped another chocolate in my mouth, 'no effort at all.'

'He's leaving a trail, remember the Maltesers in his drawer. I told you he planned it and this proves he wanted a kid to find it. Even if the police had seen that packet, adults would sooner throw away an opened bag of chocolate—who knows where it's been–than eat it like a kid like you. Even I wouldn't touch it.'

'Quite right. This is my strength.' I popped the last three in my mouth and mumbled a question.

'Please can you not talk with your mouth full?'

'Umm Um Umm, 'I swallowed, 'sorry. What do you think is on it. A map?' I asked excitedly.

'Let's return the key to miss in the canteen and we'll soon find out.'

CHAPTER EIGHT

The top of the pops

After we gave the master key back to House Matron in the canteen, and explained the locker was empty, being careful not to mention the memory stick from the bag of Maltesers, we raced to our room.

I couldn't stop thinking what might be on it. As well as a map, maybe a diary, escape plans or even a suicide note, fear tingled down my spine at the thought. I couldn't wait to get in but when we finally reached the door, Mason didn't open it.

'Did you forget your key card?'

He held up a key card. 'Room 78. We might need this to get back in, so I switched them, and gave her mine.'

'But what if she tries to use it?'

He shook his head, 'She uses a master key card for every room. And if she did, it was an accident, miss, I'm so sorry.'

I smiled, 'You are unbelievable.'

'Coming from you that's a compliment. Now hurry up and open this door. We need to find out what's on that stick.'

'I know, I know,' I let us in, held the door open for him to wheel himself in and he went straight to his laptop. I held my breath as he plugged it in, waiting for the File Explorer window to open. We were both puzzled when the files appeared and looked at each other.

'MP3 files?' he said.

'Songs.'

'I know what an MP3 file is, doctor. But I don't get it, unless ...'

'He likes music.'

'They're some kind of code. I think Patrick Mackensie is trying to sing to us. He wants us to find him and these are the clues.'

'Don't you think we should give this to The Police?'

'And say what? We found his Top 10 favourite songs. They would laugh us out of the Police Station. No, this is for us. It's a message of some kind.'

'There could be a perfectly innocent explanation.'

'Like what?' He raised his eyebrows.

'I don't know. Maybe he split up with his girlfriend and wanted to surprise her in a pack of Maltesers to win her back.'

'You are quite the old romantic, doctor, aren't you? Have your eye on any young lady you haven't told me about?'

I blushed. Of course, I did, but I wasn't about to tell him about Sarah, before I'd even asked her out. 'Don't be silly.'

'That's a yes. Blushing is a *tell*. But we must focus on the matter in hand. Just supposing it is a code—remember what isn't there, is more important than what is there—how would you hide what you wanted to say?'

'Rearrange and link the song titles into sentences?'

'Look at the list of songs, does that work?'

I read them on the screen again:

1. Centuries by Fall Out Boy

2. The Phoenix by Fall Out Boy

3. Enemy by Imagine Dragons

4. Hall of Fame by The Script

5. World's Smallest Violin by AJR

6. I'm Not Famous by AJR

7. Bang by AJR [U]

8. This Ain't a Scene, It's an Arms Race by Fall Out Boy

9. Believer by Imagine Dragons

10. Riptide by Vance Joy

'Throughout the centuries,' I said, 'the phoenix was an enemy of the hall of fame. He wasn't famous because he played the world's smallest violin until one day it went bang and he became a believer but it was too late because he was carried away by the riptide.'

Mason clapped. 'You are a romantic. Sally would love it.'

'Who said anything about Sarah?'

'See—I knew it! I said Sally, you said Sarah. You mumble when you dream. It was a fifty-fifty guess.'

'You fart when you meditate,' I said defensively.

'That's a holy fart.'

We both laughed.

'Thank goodness. You had me worried by your house rules until you did.'

'I'm sorry. But you don't know who I had to put up with until you arrived—Arthur the actor! Can you imagine? That boy's got an ego the size of the Himalayas and farts like a cyclone. To be or not to be ...' He blew a loud raspberry on the back of his hand.

We laughed.

People didn't know Mason had a sense of humour.

I don't know why he didn't share it more often, maybe it wasn't respected in his culture, or he was afraid to look ridiculous—but not with me.

'You left out the eighth song, but you haven't broken the code. Come on, try again.'

'What about alphabetically,' I said, 'the first letter of each word in the title? Let's see,' I wrote down in the back of my journal, 'C, T, E, H, W, I, B, T, B, R', and stared at the letters ... B.E.W.I.T.C.H. ... Bewitch!' I said excitedly, and then less enthusiastically, 'and T, B, R?'

'It doesn't work. Try again.'

'What about when the songs were released?' I suggested tentatively. 'Could they be coordinates?' I went to my desk, opened my laptop and searched for the first song on Wikipedia.

Centuries was released on 9th September 2014.

'I've got the first coordinates, 09092014. 'Could that be nine degrees, nine hours, twenty seconds point fourteen latitude, North? The Phoenix was released on March 24, 2013, 24032013, twenty-four degrees, three hours and twenty seconds point thirteen longitude East.'

I searched google maps.

There was a picture of a black African tribesman in white turban and scarf and long turquoise robe squatting on the sand.

'He's in Central Africa.'

'I'm sorry to disappoint you, doctor, but I don't think he would have made it to Central Africa with a school bag. Try again.'

'I give up. Why don't you tell me if you have a better idea.'

'It's obvious. Let's play the songs. They're songs after all. And don't look for the literal meaning, think about what he needs to feel by listening to them. We listen to music for a reason, don't we—at least I do—to give me something I'm missing. If it's a code, he will have chosen them from the songs he knows. Music is the door into your soul.'

He played the first song, Centuries, and I tapped my foot and nodded my head to the thumping beat and roaring chorus.

'It's a great song.'

'How does it make you feel?

This was hard. 'I don't know. Play it again.' As he did, I gave a running commentary, 'I want to escape. I don't want to be forgotten ...'

'Good. The Police won't be doing this. Go on.'

'Turn it up. Confident. I can do anything. I've got the power. The might. I've got to do it.'

'Exactly. Next one.'

He played The Phoenix.

I shook my head from side to side in time, trying to listen to my feelings. 'Turn it up. I'm really going to do it. I'm going to change this. I'm free. Nothing's going to stop me.'

'Good. Feel how he feels listening to this. Next one.'

I was really enjoying this and it didn't feel like detective work at all.

He played Enemy.

I couldn't help my shoulders lifting from side to side.

'Everyone's against me. I'm paranoid. They're all against me.'

'Good. Next one.'

He played Hall of Fame.

'Turn it up. I'm going to be famous. Everybody's going to talk about me. I've done it.'

'Excellent. Next one.' He played World's Smallest Violin.

I clicked my fingers and smiled, 'this is cool.'

'Your feelings...'

'I'm happy. Joy. Pure joy. Everything's good,' I nodded my chin, 'yeah. Next one.'

He played I'm Not Famous.

I swayed from side to side, this was better than school.

'Turn it up. I don't care. It doesn't matter if I'm famous or not. I'm doing the right thing. Everybody else is wrong.'

'Good. Your feelings remember. Next one.'

He played Bang.

I puffed my chest in and out in time to the music.

'I've made my mind up. I'm going. I can't stay. Get ready to go.'

'Good. Three more.'

He played This Ain't a Scene, It's an Arms Race.

When the chorus hit, I started banging my head up and down like a heavy-metal fan.

'I'm the man, nobody can stop me, I can do anything.'

'Good. Two more.' He played Believer.

'It's bad. I'm scared. I'm hurt ...'

There was suddenly a knock at the door and without waiting to be invited in, the House Matron popped her head around the door and I almost jumped out of my skin. Mason quickly stopped the song.

'Having a party, are we? I could hear you half way down the corridor.'

I looked at Mason and the thumb drive in the laptop. What if she realised it was Patrick Mackensie's playlist and we'd stolen his thumb drive? We were finished. Investigation over. But Mason was as quick as lightening.

'Sorry miss. I was feeling down about my father's D&D book and Alex was just trying to cheer me up.'

I nodded quickly when she looked at me.

'Just trying to take his mind off it, miss, you know.'

'What a good idea. That's very thoughtful of you, Alex. But you must be mindful of other people in the dorm who might be trying to study. How are you feeling now, Mason?'

'Much better, miss. The music really helps.'

'Of course it does. We all like a little bit of music to cheer us up sometimes, don't we?' She smiled.

She didn't suspect anything, I mean, anything.

'I'll leave you boys to your music.' She opened the door, and turned back. 'Oh, I almost forgot,' she held up a key card, 'you must have dropped this when you got out of my car?'

I shot Mason a stare but he just smiled. 'Thank you, miss.'

'Not too loud, boys.' And left.

'That was close.' I sighed, letting out a deep breath.

'Everyone makes sense of the world *their* way,' he shrugged, 'that's their weakness. That's why the police will never find Patrick Mackensie, unless we do. Come on, the last song, but take my headset.'

He played Riptide.

I heard a happy Banjo and then a lonesome lonely wail of woe about running away.

'I'm hurt, confused, I need to get away.'

It ended suddenly, a bit like Patrick Mackensie's sudden disappearance.

'Good. So, tell me what we know.'

I blew out a deep breath, 'That was heavy.'

'Can you feel Patrick Mackensie now?'

I thought about it for a moment. It was strange but it was like he was in the room while we were listening. His spirit was there in the songs somehow, or his state of mind.

'It's *him*, isn't it?'

I pictured the puppy above his desk and him sitting there listening to the songs. 'Yes, I can feel him.'

'He's trying to tell us something, isn't he?'

'Yes, I suppose he is. It's like a message from the grave.'

'Don't say that. He isn't dead yet, I hope. But what's the message?'

'I don't know. You just told me to describe how it made me feel.'

'How does it make you feel in a sentence.'

'I'm lost and lonely, I've got to get out of here and I've got to do something.'

'Exactly.'

Although we were no closer to locating his whereabouts than when we'd started and in spite of Mason's encouragement, I felt like we had reached another dead end. Mason decided to meditate while I went to sleep.

CHAPTER NINE

The treasure map

That night I had a dream, or rather nightmare.

I was running down a dark dorm corridor trying to escape someone chasing me, trying to open doors for help but they were all locked, until I reached the end of the corridor and there was nowhere to escape. Just before he reached me, I woke up startled and panting heavily.

In a half-dazed confusion, it hit me, 'they're rooms!'

I gently nudged Mason by the shoulder in the darkness and whispered, 'Wake up, wake up. I've got it.'

Mason blearily opened his eyes, which looked perfectly normal without the glasses, and looked around the room still half-asleep. 'What time is it?'

'Three-thirty. But I've got to tell you. I had a dream.'

'Good for you. Now go back to sleep.'

'No, you don't understand. I've figured it out. The songs are rooms!'

'What are you talking about?'

'That's the *code*. The message Patrick Mackensie is trying to tell us. Don't you see? Each song is a clue to a room.'

Mason sat up leaning on his elbows, wiped his eyes with his hands and put on his glasses. 'A room?'

'Think about it. Centuries, could be the History room, the Phoenix could be, I don't know, the Chemistry lab, Enemy could be ... the headmaster's office?'

'You think Patrick Mackensie is hiding in the headmaster's office?'

'Not literally. I don't know. I know it sounds crazy, but ...'

'It sounds crazy,' Mason nodded, 'go back to sleep, Alex.'

'I thought you'd be a bit more excited?'

'It's four o'clock in the morning, Alex.' He turned over and put the pillow over his head.

I shook my head, returned to my bed, and tried to get back to sleep but it took a while because I couldn't stop thinking of the possibilities.

In the morning, I woke to see Mason sitting meditating with his bandaged foot on the floor and a not so-serene smile, having forgotten the incident in the night-time until his eye suddenly opened and he said, 'I've got it. They're rooms!'

I sighed, 'That's what I *told* you.' I wasn't angry, more relieved that he agreed.

'But not the History room, the Chemistry lab, or the headmaster's office, doctor.'

I heard the bell ring for morning registration and stared at my watch in shock. I wasn't even dressed. I jumped out of the bed and scrambled into my uniform without a shower or even brushing my teeth.

'Why didn't you wake me?'

'I was meditating. You've got Harris first period for History and then Miss Hardy for English. Teachers, remember. You've got to find out what you can about Patrick Mackensie's hopes, dreams and ambitions. I'll check his grades.'

'I haven't got time for this. See you at break.' I grabbed my school bag and ran as fast as I could.

I just made it in time to see Miss Betul open her green hard-backed book and enter the login details I could have told her myself, before she started calling our names.

'You look awful.' Sarah whispered beside me.

'Thanks,' I said, and stroked my hair with my clawed fingers in lieu of a brush.

'And your breath smells.'

I looked at her in shock and she just smiled.

What did it have to do with her, I thought.

Miss Betul told us History had been cancelled for a special assembly with the headmaster.

In the Grand Hall, the headmaster in his black gown stood behind a podium on the stage with a policewoman sitting behind him.

After a long-winded reminder of our duties and responsibilities as Grangers, he said, 'It is my sad duty to report that a boy has gone missing.'

I thought he wasn't exactly quick with the news.

It had been almost three days, and by this point the whole world must have known, but pupils around me looked surprised and a murmur rose in the hall like the swell of the sea rising trying to guess who it could be.

'Patrick Mackensie in Year 7 has taken temporary leave of us, and if you have any information as to his whereabouts it is vital that your teachers know so that we can help the Police in their enquiries.'

I looked across the hall and I could see the House Matron standing behind Mason on the side of the hall, she must have wheeled him down. He looked as surprised as everyone else at the news. The House Matron looked like it was her fault and I felt a twinge of sympathy for her because it obviously wasn't.

'There is a reward of fifty-thousand pounds for any information leading directly to his recovery, which will obviously be reimbursed to your parents.'

I thought what my father would think of getting fifty-thousand pounds, when he could barely afford the taxi fare to bring me to school. It probably wouldn't mean so much to any of the rich parents of other pupils here, but to him it would be life-changing, and maybe he wouldn't argue with my mother about shopping receipts any more.

'If you know anything, however small, or insignificant you may think it is, you must let your teachers know immediately or talk to PC White, our Police School Liaison Officer.' He turned to her and she seemed torn between a frown and a smile and it came out like a grimace.

I thought about searching Patrick Mackensie's room and finding the memory stick and panicked at the thought of being arrested by her for withholding evidence.

We all stood as the headmaster led PC White down the centre aisle, and right passed me at the end of the row, my eyes fixed straight ahead as inconspicuously as possible. My legs were shaking and my hair a mess, I thought a policewoman was bound to notice, but she didn't.

'What's wrong, you look like you've seen a ghost,' Sarah said when they had left, and a general hubbub rose in the grand hall, probably about the fifty-thousand pounds.

'You could say that,' I said. I didn't say I could sense one in his room, which was closer to the truth, and quickly changed the topic.

'Did you know Patrick Mackensie?'

'That creep, me? I think he fancied me. Are you jealous?'

I laughed.

'What was he like ... I mean, what is he like?'

'Not my type. Good at art.'

'I know,' I said before immediately regretting it, but she didn't seem to notice.

'He liked animals.'

'Imagine dragons?'

She gave me a strange look, 'No, drawing animals. I don't know what music he was into.'

'Me neither.' I tried to remember what Mason had told me to ask his teachers. 'What about his hopes, dreams and ambitions?'

'What about yours? If you're thinking about the fifty-grand, forget it. If they haven't found him by now, nobody will.'

The Head of Year reached our row and we all stood and I led the row out in single file, feeling like I had failed at my first interview with a witness.

Back in the dorm room, Mason was eager to know exactly what Sarah had said, but I didn't have much to report.

'He liked drawing animals, which we already know, and he fancied her. Oh yeah, and my breath smells.'

'Bad luck old chap,' he smiled.

I looked down. I wasn't thinking about Patrick Mackensie's failed chance with her, or my own, but I felt sorry for Mason. What girl was ever going to be interested in him, I thought, a frail Indian boy with one eye and fat glasses. He didn't have any self-pity, though, except for that one time.

'Don't look down,' he said, 'there's always hope, remember.'

'There's always hope.' I swallowed and felt silly for being emotional about it when it clearly didn't seem to worry him. Although I bet it must hurt him when nobody's looking, or would, when everyone else was getting valentine's cards or trying to get a dance at a party. I changed the topic quickly.

'Did you find out his grades?'

Mason tapped on his keyboard and all Patrick Mackensie's grades and behaviour report appeared.

'A for Art, no surprises there, and A for Latin but all the rest are D's and E's ... But this is interesting. He won the annual Year 6 headmaster's prize last year. He must have worked his butt off to gain those house points. Who else bothers, right?'

'I don't know, I wasn't here.'

'It means he cared, I mean, really cared.

'You have to jump through every loop, term after term, to get those points. I know it isn't academic, but this kid was trying to do his best. You look at his grades and you think what a loser, but he wasn't in his mind. To him, he was the best.'

'But how does that help us find him?'

'I'm coming to that, give me a chance. How would you feel if one minute you're the top of the Year and the next you're failing at everything. They build you up just to knock you down. Wouldn't that make you angry at who?

'The injustice of the school.

'To him, he's brilliant, it isn't *his* fault, it's the system.

'The very system he had played so well.

'Who knows how proud his parents must have been when he won the headmaster's prize, or what bribes they rewarded him with.

'Self-esteem is a very fragile thing at our age, don't I know it. He didn't need to do an entrance test, like you, last term, because we are already at the school. If he had, maybe it would have been a wake-up call.

'But he was suddenly hit with failure as soon as the year started, and the work got harder and went up a level. That must have been devastating to him precisely *because* he won the headmaster's prize.'

'Are you saying it would have been better if he didn't win the headmaster's prize?'

'In a way, yes. He's an artist, he's obviously a sensitive soul, like you.'

'Me?'

'Oh, come on, it's me you're talking to, Alex. Have you forgotten your first week here, already?'

It seemed so long ago. But no, I hadn't forgotten crying myself to sleep. 'That doesn't mean I'm sensitive.'

'Whatever you say. But he definitely was. Remember the songs? You still don't think he's sensitive? Most boys our age listen to happy-go lucky pop, not Enemy or Bang by AJR.'

'What about the rooms?'

'It's a map.'

'A map?'

'Like a treasure map. You were right. They will lead us to him, I'm certain, if he's still alive. Hurry, and push this thing. There isn't much time.'

'You haven't told me where we're going?'

'I'll tell you on the way. Quick, open that door.'

Chapter Ten

The first clue

I wheeled Mason down the corridor ever harder at his constant urging to go faster, like my repeated requests to turn the music up.

'It came to me when I was meditating.'

'It usually does,' I said out of the corner of my mouth, not entirely kindly.

'Centuries. What is the symbol of centuries in this school?'

It was a squeeze with the wheelchair but we got in the staff lift.

'I don't know. I said our history room, but you said that's wrong.'

'The oldest part of this building, of course. The foundation cornerstone at the bottom of the front-left tower. There's a bronze plaque above it, didn't they show you on your tour?'

I tried to remember the tour, but it was so long ago it was like a different world. The lift doors opened on the ground floor.

'Never mind. You'll have one now. Come on.'

I pushed him out through the main entrance and along the path, manicured front lawns to our left, flowerbeds underneath the high tall windows to our right, until we reached the tower. There was a bronze plaque on the giant rock brickwork, which seemed to be disintegrating with the years, and I stepped over the rope and onto the soil, wary of leaving footprints, to read it, '"Herein lies the cornerstone of our greatness for centuries to come."

Centuries, it says *centuries*,' I repeated excitedly before finishing, "May it shed light on our darkness and be a tribute to the values we hold as firm.'

'Yes, I remember it, why didn't I think. What now? How do we know this is the right spot?'

'He would have to leave us a sign. There must be something here.'

'Where?' I looked around the corner and back the way we'd come along the path. 'There's nothing here.'

'I can't reach. Dig below the sign.'

'I haven't got a shovel.'

'Use your hands, this is important.'

'Fine, but I better not be getting my hands dirty for nothing.'

I gingerly stuck my right fingers into the soil under the sign and pulled up handfuls of dirt. A purple worm wiggled out of the roots as I crumpled the soil. Little rocks dropped out, 'there's nothing.'

'What's that?' He pointed to a small pile of rocks that had fallen out. I couldn't see anything.

'That,' he pointed more urgently, 'there! It's not a rock.'

I lowered onto my haunches to look more closely. He was right, one of the small rocks was wrapped in something, and handed it to him.

He carefully unpeeled the layer, and opened it out.

It looked like a torn piece of paper from a dictionary, but as if that wasn't surprising enough, it was wrapped around a small brown ball.

'Is that what I think it is,' I said, 'can I see?'

He handed it to me. 'Let me check.' I popped it into my mouth and crunched. 'Maltesers!'

'You are disgusting.'

'I love my work. What? I'm hungry.'

'Wait a second,' he turned the torn paper over, 'there's more. It's torn from a Latin dictionary, *Non est vestrum erit flagitium.*'

'Vos, vestrum, vestri, vobis, vos, vobis,' I said, 'genitive: of you. I don't know what flagitium means.'

'It's your fault.'

'No, it's not, the teacher hasn't covered that in class yet.'

'No,' Mason shook his head. 'That's what the phrase means: It's. Your. Fault.'

I looked at Mason and a chill ran down my spine. And we both mouthed the same letters to each other, 'O.M.G.'

CHAPTER ELEVEN

The negotiation

B ack in our dorm room I paced the floor arguing with Mason, 'We've got to give this to the police. We are going to be in so much trouble.'

'And say what? We found a torn scrap of paper from an old school Latin book in the mud?'

'UNDERNEATH the cornerstone, wrapped around a MALTESER! It's got to be HIM.'

'Can you keep your voice down, someone might hear us.'

'This is INSANE!' I said in my loudest whisper. 'You're crazy, I'm crazy, Patrick Mackensie is off the charts. We're going to get expelled. Never mind, 'Non est vestrum erit flagitium', what about *Mea culpa*—it's my fault!'

'Will you please calm down, Alex. Nobody is going to be expelled.'

'How can you just sit there and say that. The voice from the dead is calling us: it's our fault. I'm going to the House Matron and telling her everything.'

'No, he's saying it's the school's fault. Don't you see? We can't stop now. He needs us. Do you want to know the truth? I can't do this without you.'

There was a knock at the door.

'Oh no,' I panicked, my heart thumping in my chest, 'it's the House Matron or the police! Someone must have seen us outside.'

'Just relax. She would have just come in. Whoever it is, let me do the talking. COME IN?'

I held my breath as the door slowly opened and a teasing girl's voice said, 'Are you decent?' Sarah's head popped around the door, and when she saw me, she smiled, 'pity.'

'What are you doing in the boy's dorm?' I asked.

She sat on Mason's bed without asking. 'I saw you wheeling him outside past the biology lab.'

'I told you someone had seen us,' I stared at Mason.

'What were you looking for?'

'I told you to keep it down,' he said. 'Nothing but there will be. We were planting rhododendrons for Miss Baxter.'

'In October?'

'They're evergreen. All year round. A lovely pink blossom.'

'Why did you ask me about Patrick Mackensie's hopes, dreams and ambitions?' She turned to me like I was the weakest link.

'You didn't use those exact words, did you?' Mason asked me.

'You told me to.'

'What is going on here? I know you're hiding something. You're blushing Alex. I promise I won't tell anyone. Girl scout honour.'

I looked at Mason shaking his head. 'No way. We can't trust a girl,' he said.

'Excuse me?' She said, 'I am sitting here you know. Who do you trust the most in the world, isn't your mum a girl?'

'You're right,' I said, 'say you're sorry, Mason.'

'I'm sorry. And I'm also sorry this is none of your business.'

'Fine,' she stood up, 'I'll just have to ask Miss Baxter if she needs any more volunteers to plant Rhododendrons outside.'

'Be my guest,' said Mason.

'Wait,' I said, 'listen Mason, she might be useful.'

'She's just after the reward money.'

'No, I'm not! How rude? My mother is the CEO of a bank. We don't need money.'

'We could use a secretary?' I suggested.

'That's sexist! I'm not anybody's secretary, thank you very much, Alex.'

Mason leaned forward in his wheelchair and fixed her with his eye, 'You have to swear absolute secrecy on your mother's life that nothing leaves this room.'

'I swear. But I'm an equal partner and it's a three-way split.'

'You just said you didn't need the money,' I said.

'That was before he made it conditional.'

'Ten per cent,' Mason said, 'We've already done ninety percent of the work.'

'Which means you've done ten percent of the work and expect me to help you do ninety. A third of ninety is thirty percent. That's the best I can do. Take it or leave it.'

'She's being fair. We've only found one out of ten of the clues, which is ten percent,' I said to Mason, 'be honest.'

'And what can you bring to the table' he steepled his fingers, 'besides a threat, for twenty percent?'

He was talking like we'd already won the reward, which was frankly, a little optimistic, especially when I'd wanted to stop before Sarah turned up, but this might be a way to impress her with more than my bad breath.

'I've got straight A's. I'm Captain of the under-13's girl's hockey team. I've got a horse, three dogs, two cats, a parrot, two hamsters and a llama. And I am going to be a vet which is harder than getting into medical school, Miss Baxter says, but she said if anyone can, I can. And I've got feminine intuition so I can find out things without holding up a giant signpost, 'hopes, dreams and ambitions' giving the game away. What do you bring to the table for thirty-five percent?'

'He meditates,' I said, 'and farts.'

Sarah laughed which brightened up the whole room. Even though he's my best friend, being with Mason can be a bit intense sometimes. I liked Sarah. I hadn't even considered asking Mason how we'd split any reward we won.

Mason rubbed his chin seeming to weigh up her usefulness, or the cut, with a poker face. 'Thirty percent without voting rights,

Alex and I have the final decision with seventy percent between us. We did start this together.'

'With voting rights but if you both agree on a decision, I'll respect the majority decision, of course.'

'Even if you disagree?'

'A deal's a deal.'

Mason held out his hand and Sarah shook it excitedly like she'd won the reward already.

I stood up and held my hand out to congratulate her, too, but she put her hands on my shoulder and gave me a peck on the cheek.

I froze like a statue and felt my heart flutter and a weird tingling feeling.

'You must negotiate harder, Mason, I would have settled for twenty-five percent. Now tell me what you were really doing outside.'

'It's too late, anyway. Alex wants to quit and tell everything to the House Matron. I can't stop him. You can go with him.'

'No, I don't. It was just a shock.'

'What was a shock?' Sarah's eyes opened wider. She took me by the hand and sat on my bed. 'Tell me, tell me, tell me.'

When I had finished explaining, and showed her the torn piece of paper, Mason scrunched up his nose, 'he actually *ate* the Malteser. Can you believe that?'

'What's this scribble?' She asked, examining the paper.

'It's just a scratch from a biro,' I said.

'Pupils don't scribble on their textbooks. It could be an E? But there's not much point in going to the Police if you ate the evidence, Alex. This can't be the first ever Latin textbook torn up and thrown out of the window over the years from an ancient public school like The Grange. There are probably hundreds of scraps buried in the soil. What is the next song?' Sarah asked. 'I love this.'

I showed her my journal and said, 'The Phoenix by Fall Out Boy.'

'Can you play it?'

'Sure. Go on Mason. Turn it up.'

The heavy violins drilled the air, the infectious beat filling the room, and I started to nod my head in time and Sarah was nodding too, her blonde ponytail bouncing on her neck, and clicking her fingers. At the chorus she suddenly jumped up and pulled me to my feet and we started dancing. I couldn't believe it. Sarah was hopping up and down, her tartan skirt flying above her knees, and punching the air with her fists. Mason was even nodding and rolling his wheelchair from side to side, and then she took his hands and danced with him. That was really nice of her, she wanted to include him, and I clapped alongside. I don't know why we hadn't danced before, it was like Sarah made us feel free.

When the song finished, Sarah asked him to play it again, but Mason refused. 'We need to find the room. Patrick Mackensie's life is at stake. But which room? What is the significance of a Phoenix?'

I jumped to my desk and googled it.

'A phoenix is an immortal bird from Greek mythology associated with the sun, which gains new life by rising from the ashes of its predecessor.'

'I know what a Phoenix is, but which room?' Mason urgently insisted.

'The sun rises in the East, could it be the East wing?' Sarah asked.

'No, there are too many rooms on the East wing, it needs to be a specific room related to ...'

'Greek mythology?' I interrupted him. 'It's obvious. The Latin room. It's on the East wing. You're brilliant Sarah.'

'You, too!' She gave me a high five.

'Come on, let's go.' Mason said.

CHAPTER TWELVE

The Latin room

S arah insisted on taking turns pushing Mason to the Latin room as an equal member of the team, which I had to respect, and although it made me feel a bit unmanly, he seemed to enjoy it more.

When we arrived, we were in luck because the room was empty but I didn't know where to start to look from the whiteboard, to the teacher's desk to the rows of wooden tables with their lift up lids and chairs to all the bookcases around the wall.

'It's impossible,' I said, 'it will take us all day to search this room, and there's a lesson next period,' I checked my watch, 'we've only got ten minutes.'

'Not now there's three of us.' Sarah said. 'I'll start where he used to sit. You try the teacher's desk and Mason search the bookcase with the dictionaries.'

'Who put you in charge?' Mason asked sorely.

'Just do it.' Sarah rushed to Patrick Mackensie's desk and opened the lid. 'I think the Police have already been here. It's empty.'

'The teacher's drawer is locked I can't get in,' I said.

'I can't reach the top shelf,' Mason said.

'Let me help you,' Sarah said and started passing dictionaries down to Mason to clear the shelf.

I absent-mindedly picked up a pupil's exercise book from the top of a stack on the desk and opened it and then suddenly had an idea. What if he's written something in his Latin exercise book? And searched the stack for Patrick Mackensie's book.' But on every grey cover, there were only random names from another form above the school coat of arms.

'There's nothing here.' Sarah said.

'His book's not here either.' I said disappointingly, holding up one of the exercise books, 'Jackson Smith, know him?' I flicked through the book. 'Doesn't know his dative from his genitive. D minus.'

Sarah laughed but Mason wheeled himself over, 'Wait a second. What was that on the cover?' He grabbed an exercise book. 'The school coat of arms. Of course. It's right there. The Phoenix is in the top right-hand quadrant, like on your blazer. How could we miss it?'

'My goodness, you've got a good eye if you can see it from over there.'

'There are hundreds of exercise books with the school crest,' Sarah said, 'and hundreds of blazers. That doesn't exactly help.'

'But only one original,' Mason said, 'hanging in the School Reception between the honours' boards! We walked right past it when we went to the cornerstone.'

A loud voice suddenly boomed across the room, 'What on earth are you doing here?' Mr Meecher, the Latin teacher, said. 'And what have you done to all my dictionaries?'

'I'm sorry, sir. I've lost my Latin dictionary, and I thought it might be here. They were just trying to help.'

'I'll put them right back,' Sarah said, putting them back on the shelf.

'And what are you doing with my marking? Don't tell me, trying to find out your grades, no doubt.'

I quickly tidied the pile. 'That's right, sir,' I said, 'I'm so sorry.'

'I should give you all a behaviour point for this mess.'

'Please, sir, it won't happen again,' Mason said, 'it's been hard getting around with my injury.'

'Let this be your first and last warning. Now go!'

I wheeled Mason out, and Sarah followed with her head down, as if not wanting her face to be remembered.

Outside the room, I let out a sigh of relief.

'That was close.'

'What are you stopping for?' Mason said impatiently, 'to Reception, a.s.a.p.!'

CHAPTER THIRTEEN

Coat of arms

We arrived in Reception and looked up at the large Coat of Arms on the wall, and I suddenly remembered Elvis showing it to us on the tour. What did he say? 'The Unicorn represents power and the Phoenix represents resurrection, I think.'

'Purity, innocence and power.' Sarah corrected me.

'And resurrection?' Mason said, almost to himself.

'So, where's the Malteser? I'm famished.'

'How are we going to get up there?' Sarah asked. 'With a ladder?'

Visitors entered through the front doors and spoke through the window to Miss Lavender, the young lady on reception.

'He wouldn't have been able to get a ladder in here unnoticed. Where is the herald pointing?'

'Straight down,' I said.

We all looked down at the black and white tiled floor and there was a little three-inch square wooden lid cut into the corner of one black tile, with an antique brass flush ring pull embedded in it.

I looked at Mason, and he nodded, and then Sarah, and she nodded.

'Cover me', I said and casually walked over to the plate, while they shaded me as I bent down on one knee as if to tie my shoelaces, and making sure nobody was looking, lifted the ring pull with one finger and pulled up the wooden plate.

I saw a boxed-in brass tap, which I guessed must be for gas, and there underneath a small ball barely visible in the dark hole.

I clawed my hand around the tap and finally pincered the ball between my fore and index fingers and carefully raised it out, and lowered the lid down.

'Got it!' I whispered and Sarah half-turned with this huge grin on her face.

We shuffled out of reception back into the school as casually as possible, trying to hide the joy on our faces, because pupils never looked this happy about entering the school.

We caught the staff lift to the dorm and ran the wheelchair down the corridor to our room with Mason crying, 'Faster'.

We closed the door, and Sarah and I were panting as I pulled the small ball out of my pocket. I unwrapped the paper and sure enough there was another Malteser. It pained me, but good manners forced me, to offer it to Sarah.

'I think you deserve it more than me,' she said, 'but give me the paper.'

'No, give it to me,' Mason said.

I handed it to her and gleefully popped the chocolate in my mouth. I closed my eyes to savour the taste. Oh, it was delicious, infinitely delicious beyond deliciousness.

Mason looked glum as Sarah read it with a confused frown before handing it to him. 'It's torn from a Latin dictionary, I don't know what it means but there's another squiggle across it, like an R?'

Mason read aloud, '*Mortuum flagellas*,' and then looked up with a long, pained face, 'it means, you are flogging a dead man.'

We were too stunned to speak and, in the silence, the gravity of the statement seemed to weigh me physically down and my legs felt weak. I dropped onto my bed.

'I've got to go.' Sarah said.

'Not a word,' Mason said, 'you promised.'

Sarah shook her head and drew a zip across her lips, 'I promise. Bye. Bye, Alex. '

'Oh, yeah. Sorry, bye.'

'Try not to worry,' she left.

Then it was just the two of us with this awful weight to carry and neither of us wanting to talk about the elephant in the room; what if he's dead?

Chapter Fourteen

Reincarnation or resurrection

T hat night as I lay in bed after lights out, I watched the moon
rising through the gap in the curtain and asked Mason,
'What happens when you die?'

'It's no big deal. You just get born again.'

'How?'

'It's like a cycle. The sun evaporates the sea, the water in the air
rises up a mountain, the air cools and the rain falls, and runs back
down in a river to the sea.

'Or a Chestnut tree drops a chestnut and it falls to the ground
and becomes a seed and grows branches and leaves and drops
another chestnut.

'We are born, we grow up, we get married, have a baby, we die
and it starts all over again.

'The only difference is depending on how good you are in your last life determines the life you get in the next one. It's called Karma. You could come back as anything and you keep coming back until you reach enlightenment, so it all works out in the end.'

'My mother says we go to heaven or hell depending on whether we're good or bad,' I said, 'but my father doesn't believe in hell. He says God is love and a loving God wouldn't send anyone to hell if he understands everyone and everything. He says hell is this life if we do something wrong, but I suppose he would. My mother told me he went to prison when I was very little. Promise you won't tell anyone. He doesn't know I know.'

'Of course not. What did he do, murder?'

'Fraud. He lied to the Police when he was a bookkeeper, I think he was doing research for a book, but the Judge obviously didn't see it that way. That's why he can't get a job as an accountant.'

'I'm not surprised. It must be really hard for you, I'm sorry.'

'Not really, I still love my dad, except when he drinks. That is hell. It's like he wants to kill himself and blames my mum for everything. Do your parents argue?'

'Everyone's parents argue. I don't know why they got married in the first place. It's all about opposites. Pain and pleasure. Hot and cold. You've got to find the middle way.'

'What do your parents argue about?'

'Me, mostly!' He snorted like it was a joke. 'I was born twelve weeks prematurely and I developed amblyopia. My father blames my mum, and vice versa. That's why I wear a patch on my good eye.'

'On your *good* eye? That doesn't make sense.'

'It's to strengthen my weak eye. Otherwise, they said my brain will just focus on my good eye and I'll lose sight in my weak eye. It's like my little secret. Everyone thinks I can't see out of this eye because of my patch, but the opposite is true. People always jump to the wrong assumption.'

'That's weird. I would never have guessed. I'm so sorry.'

'It's nothing. It's always been there, I don't know any different.'

'Is that why you were seeing a counsellor?'

'No. We should try and sleep, Alex. We've got a lot to do in the morning. And we've got to find out which room is Enemy.'

'I've been thinking, it could be ...'

'Goodnight Alex. In the morning.'

'Goodnight Mason, sweet dreams.'

I was disappointed because I had a brilliant idea, and I was certain I knew which room it was, but I rolled over and tried to sleep.

Why does night time seem to go so much slower than day time, I thought. I couldn't wait till morning to tell him.

CHAPTER FIFTEEN

The Enemy

I chomped through my cornflakes sitting opposite Mason eating a yoghurt in the canteen, the bright sunlight through the high windows glinting off his spectacles, when Sarah came over with her tray, with a slice of toast, honey and an apple.

'Mind if I join you, have you solved the next riddle?'

'Mason doesn't think I have,' I said sorely. She sat beside me.

'Enemy is not going to be a teacher,' Mason said.

'But he said, you're flogging a dead man, who is flogging him then? It has to be a teacher. Maybe he had a detention and wanted revenge.'

'Can I hear the song?'

Mason handed her his iPhone, he had downloaded all the songs onto it, and I shared an earpiece with her as Enemy by Imagine Dragons played.

I heard the infectious reggae beat and started heaving my chest out again in time, and when I looked over, Sarah was doing the same, and for a split second I noticed it was her bosom rising and falling and quickly looked straight at Mason, feeling guilty of the observation, and hoping she hadn't noticed me staring.

I tried to concentrate on the song for a clue. He was singing the whole world was against him. The whole world to him was the school. It had to be a teacher. The song suddenly stopped.

'It's a girl,' Sarah said.

I looked at her like she had just said aliens had landed, 'A girl?'

'Are boys that dumb? Of course, it's about a relationship gone wrong. It's obvious. Don't tell me you've never had your heart broken before, or broken a few hearts yourself, someone as good-looking as you.'

Mason winked at me with his weak eye.

'Don't you think he's good looking, Mason?' She must have seen the wink.

'He's not my type.'

'Me, good-looking?'

Sarah shook her head as if she didn't believe me.

'Don't be modest. All the girls talk about how cute Alex is, and how kind you are, and what a gentleman you are, and Alex this and Alex that.'

'Are you winding me up?'

She raised her eyebrows at Mason, 'Now he's fishing for compliments.'

'Can we please focus on the enemy, rather than how good-looking or not Alex is? A boy's life is at stake here, not Alex's sex life.'

'Sorry, but it's true, and I tell them they've got no chance, but not why,' she said mysteriously.

'Thanks,' I said sarcastically, 'I'll do the same for you sometime.'

'The *enemy*, everyone, please?'

'Sorry, unrequited love.' Sarah said.

'You've got love on the brain,' I said, 'it's got to be a teacher, Mason.' Just then the House Matron appeared behind Mason's wheelchair.

'And I want to be the wizard,' I said quickly.

'A wizard? What are you talking about?' Mason said.

'Good morning pupils, how are we all today? Nothing gets past me, you know.' She squinted her eye, and for a moment I thought she knew everything. 'Did I hear someone say, wizard? Nice to see you, Sarah. Did you find your D&D book, Mason?'

'I'd fed up of being a troll,' Sarah said, sharp as a playing card.

'No, miss, discussing our favourite D&D characters.'

'It doesn't seem very kind of you boys making Sarah a troll if she doesn't want to be. She's Captain of the under-13 girls' hockey team, you know. She should be the Queen.'

'There isn't a queen in dungeons and dragons, miss,' I said.

'Then there should be. Like me,' she giggled, 'not really. How's the foot, Mason?'

'Much better, thanks. I don't think I need the chair any more, if I can just get this bandage off, I can walk fine.'

'Let the doctor be the judge of that. I just came over to remind you, you're seeing him at two this afternoon in the sick bay. Have a lovely day. Don't forget, two pm. Goodbye.'

Mason watched her leave, and then said urgently, 'we haven't got much time. Who's Patrick Mackensie's biggest enemy? It's not a girl, boys our age don't think like girls. And it's not a teacher. If it was, he'd try and get back at them personally. It's the whole school that's his enemy, the system. I told you before, he won the headmaster's prize and then he flunked almost everything.'

'Except Art and Latin,' I explained to Sarah.

'What was trying to flog him? All his grades. And where are his grades stored?'

'On the school database.'

'And where is the school database?'

'On every computer, you know that,' I said, 'but everyone's got a laptop. We can't check them all.'

'The school database is on a server. There's only one server in the whole school. It's in the admin block, in a separate room beside the sickbay, I saw Mr Franks, the IT technician go in while I was waiting after my accident. I lifted my eye patch and I saw him press the metal buttons on the lock, each from the top left diagonally, and then each from the top right diagonally. You never know when this may be useful. The door opened and it was like a little cupboard inside with a big metal box with all these wires coming out.'

'You lifted your eyepatch?' Sarah asked disbelievingly, 'the one you can't see out of?'

'That's his good eye,' I explained, 'it's a long story. But we don't know anything about servers.'

'We don't need to. Nor does Patrick Mackensie. We just need to find the note.'

'And the Malteser, don't forget the Maltesers!'

'But what reason do we have for going to the Server room?' I said.

Mason pointed at his foot. 'We're going to the sick bay. I've got an appointment at 9.30am.'

'I thought she said 2pm.'

'We don't want to be there when it's open, do we? It opens in thirty minutes. Come on, there isn't much time.'

We all stood up, including Mason, and then he stopped. 'Oh, I forgot,' he sat down again, 'push me.'

And we all rushed off to the server room.

CHAPTER SIXTEEN

The server room

The sickbay room door was open, as always, but empty with a sign on the door with the opening hours 10am to 3pm, Mason was right.

We just needed to keep an eye on the short corridor while Mason entered the security code on the Server room door, which seemed to magically open.

We all squeezed in after Mason, and I closed the door behind us.

I was pressing up against Sarah's back and I felt her bottom suddenly gently press back against my crotch in the pitch-black darkness, and I prayed she didn't feel me becoming aroused, trying to repeat second declensions of 'the bear' to take my mind off it: ursus, ursī, ursum, urse, ursī, ursō. Why I thought of bears, I have no idea.

'Get the light,' Mason whispered.

I felt along the side of the door with my hand and finally found the switch. The room lit up and I gasped with relief, blaming claustrophobia in my mind, but I knew it wasn't what I was scared of.

'Where do we start?' Sarah said.

'That's the server,' he said pointing to the stacked black computers, with red and blue leads plugged into each other, with a monitor and router on top with two antennae, and a small table lamp on top, surrounded by a large grey steel box on three sides with holes an inch wide.

'It must be here somewhere,' Mason said.

We all turned in different directions and reached over one another like in a game of twister, and I couldn't help rubbing up against Sarah in all the wrong places but she just laughed, 'hey, no tickling, Alex.'

'That wasn't me,' I said and saw Mason smiling to himself.

I stopped and stared at the grey metal surround; the holes were the size of maltesers.

'Sarah, get up. Can you reach that table lamp and turn it on. Good. One second, I'm going to turn the lights off, and watch the walls and floor.'

I turned the light off, and suddenly the room outside the box was painted in a pattern of little lights of polka dot.

'Very pretty,' Sarah said, 'now what?'

'Look for a dot that's missing, the size of a Malteser blocking one of the holes.'

'That one!' Mason cried pointing to the wall just to the left of the box.

I traced the rays and counted the rows, 'it must be jammed into the hole on the left of the third shelf. Can you see it, Sarah?'

'Wait a second, yes,' she stretched her arm out. 'I can feel something ... I've got it!' She pulled her arm in and rubbed her armpit, 'oww, that hurt.'

'Give it to me, quick!' Mason said.

'No,' Sarah said, 'it was my arm.'

She unwrapped the paper around the little ball which sure enough to my delight was another Malteser. I frowned at the thought of it in her hands, and my treasure disappearing. But she said, 'here you go, Alex. Your reward, my knight-errant.'

'Awesome,' I popped the little piece of heaven into my mouth and savoured the taste of melting chocolate on my tongue and relished the crunch of the honeycomb biscuit centre. Whatever may be said about Patrick Mackensie, he had very good taste.

'What does it say?' Mason asked, a little sourly, clearly not enjoying someone else reading it.

'There's another squiggle, it can't be a coincidence, but it isn't clear. It could be a G? The first letter was E, the second, R, ... E.R.G.? But that can't be a word. Nothing starts with E.R.G.? Perhaps I'm wrong, I need to look at the other notes again.'

'What about ergonomic?' I said.

'That's only nine letters. There are ten songs. Ten letters.'

'It could be a Latin word,' Mason said, 'but there are lots of words beginning E.R.G. in Latin. The dictionary's full of them. Is it torn from a Latin dictionary?'

'Yes, sorry, I assumed you'd know, but I don't know what it means.' She handed it to Mason.

She must have a thing about squiggles, like tea reading, it could be anything, whereas I just wanted to know the message and wished she had handed it to Mason in the first place. She was slowing us down.

I watched Mason's eye in the thick lens trace from left to right, trying to read his expression, hoping it would be some good news, or at least not as catastrophic as the last two.

When he looked up, he seemed puzzled, like he didn't understand.

'*Cui bono* ...'

'I know that,' I said, 'Cui means to whom/to which, relative, and bono means good. Who's good?'

'That's the literal translation, but I think it's an expression, 'good' in the sense of 'advantage'. Like, *who benefits*?'

'Can we please get out of here now, we're going to be late for Music,' Sarah said, 'and if I'm found in a broom closet with two boys, I'll never hear the end of it.'

'Alex, open the door a fraction and check the coast is clear, don't just jump out.'

I carefully opened the door enough to see down the corridor.

'All clear,' I said.

We all tumbled out of the room, and I tried to push Mason as casually as possible down the busy main corridor, with pupils coming and going in heated debates about nothing important, like football or grades, and teachers laboured under the weight of their esoteric subject knowledge to classes which they thought was everything.

We still had a missing boy to find. That was the difference between us and them; we *cared* about Patrick Mackensie. We just had to find him.

Chapter Seventeen

Hall of Fame

We were late for music, and Miss Cathlewaite sarcastically welcomed us, as we tried to surreptitiously take our seats, 'how nice of you three to join us? Behaviour points for Mason, Alex and Sarah,' she noted in her laptop on top of the grand piano she was seated at.

'I am surprised it's you, Sarah. As I was saying, the picture we have of Mozart is all wrong with the wig and angelic face. Mozart, in fact, suffered awfully from the way he looked. He was only five feet tall, with a huge protruding nose, a disfigured-by-smallpox face, and deformed ears ...'

'A bit like you,' I heard a whisper and turned to see Charlie nudge Mason. I wanted to run over and punch his face in.

'But they were remarkably acute ears. He wrote his first symphony at nine years old, only three years younger than you, and we all know his famous tunes like, 'Dum. Dum-dum.

Dum-dum-dum-dum-dum-dah? Does anybody remember what it's called, hands up? Sarah.'

'Eine Kleine Nachtmusik.'

'That's right.' She played it on the piano. 'Now do you know this one, da-da-da-da-der, da-da-da-da-der, dadadader-dadadader-dadadader-der?'

I hadn't a clue, but Sarah nudged me and pointed at the back of her exercise book, where she'd written, Turkish March.

'Alex?'

'Is it Turkish March, miss?'

'Excellent, Alex. The third movement of Mozart's eleventh piano sonata in A major called Rondo Alla Turca, which is why we know it as the Turkish march.' She played the first section, and I couldn't believe I recognised it, while Sarah wrote, 'what is the next song?'

'I wrote underneath, 'Hall of Fame by The Script.'

'Notice how the first and second phrases are like a statement and answer. Statement,' she played the first bar again, 'and answer,' she played the second bar. 'And then we switch to A minor and we get the statement', she played it, which sounded exactly the same but slightly lower, 'and answer. But here's the really great thing. At the same time as we have statement and answer in the phrases, we have a statement in the C major part, and the A minor part is an answer.'

'What's the answer?' Sarah wrote.

'And this is such a great feature of music generally that it operates on so many layers simultaneously.'

'Grand Hall?' I wrote.

'And then we get the first part again but it has a different ending. This is the augmented sixth chord ...'

Sarah crossed it out and wrote, 'Likes music. Concert Hall?'

'Just a quick reminder of theory. The augmented sixth is on the sixth scale degree, and if it's in minor it's the sixth, so,' she played the broken chord, 'and if it's in major you need to have the flattened sixth ...'

I crossed out Sarah's suggestion and wrote, 'Not classical! Sports Hall=Fame.'

'... It's always the minor sixth from the root. So, it's an f here in a minor and then you add a seventh to the f, which is spelt as an augmented sixth ...'

Sarah crossed it out, and wrote, 'Hates sport—he's an artist!'

I looked at her with my jaw wide open and wrote, 'the headmaster's trophy is in the trophy cabinet outside the art room!' And her eyes lit up without having to write a word.

'...In effect,' Miss Cathlewaite seemed to get confused, 'it's a seventh but it's an augmented sixth, and err, then you add an A as the third, this is the root of the augmented sixth, and then you have the different nationalities, like the Italian, French or German but we're not going into that, because I can see I've already lost some of you. Alex and Sarah, am I interrupting you two lovebirds?'

There were giggles from the class at our expense.

'No, miss,' Sarah said taking more offence than I and as if on the attack, 'that's the Italian you just played, and if you add the C you have the full seventh German chord, or if you add a B, instead of the C, you get the French sixth chord.'

'If you know it better than I, and really don't need to pay attention, perhaps you'd like to play it for us?' She said it like a threat.

'Fine,' Sarah stood, walked to the piano and sat down, calling Miss Cathlewaite's bluff.

Miss Cathlewaite was so surprised and embarrassed she pulled off the sheet music she'd been following and said, 'By ear!'

The class collectively drew in a gasp of surprise, while Sarah calmly massaged each hand with her thumb, and then corrected the height of the stool. She sat with her back perfectly straight, and composed herself with a deep breathe, and began to play so beautifully and precisely with such swiftness and dexterity, tone and depth, I could have cried.

When she finished the whole class spontaneously clapped, which is more than they had done for Miss Cathlewaite's rendition. And after the lesson, when the class was leaving, she stopped Sarah by the arm.

'Sarah, I'm so sorry for saying lovebirds. You're quite right, it is none of my business. You play beautifully. I'm curious how you know it so well?'

'That's OK. I did it for my Grade 8, miss.'

'Yes, yes, of course.'

'What about her behaviour points, miss?' I said, 'doesn't she deserve some credit for playing to the class?'

She heaved a sigh and then her face turned stern again and turning her back on us, she said, 'Don't ever be late for my lesson again. I'll remove them for you both this once, and you can thank

Sarah for that. Now hurry on to your next lesson, or you'll be late for that too!'

We thanked her and left before she changed her mind.

Miss Cathlewaite was nice, she just wasn't very good on piano.

Mason was waiting for us outside and we both couldn't wait to tell him.

'You can tell him,' I said.

'You go ahead,' Sarah said generously, 'it was your idea.'

'Can anyone please tell what you're going on about?'

'The Hall of Fame. It's the trophy cabinet outside the art room.'

'I knew it. That's exactly what I was thinking. Break finishes in fifteen minutes. Let's go.'

CHAPTER EIGHTEEN

The trophy cabinet

We stood in front of the glass antique trophy cabinet filled with huge silver academic, sporting, art and music cups and there in the centre was the silver headmaster's cup, with the years and names of each winner starting in 1999 with Gareth Henderson and ending last year with Patrick Mackensie. He really had won it. He was the last pupil you would expect to have gone missing.

I pulled one of the two knobs on the front. 'It's locked.'

'Of course, it's locked,' Mason said, 'you didn't expect them to leave the door of the crown jewels open.'

'Maybe it's outside around here somewhere.' I looked down at the empty wall-to-wall cream carpeted floor between the ornate legs, and behind, the back was attached to the wall. I examined the keyhole beside the knobs, 'it's a very old lock, do you think we could pick it?'

'This isn't the movies, Alex,' Sarah said, 'how could he have got in?'

'The only person that would have been able to get in without arousing suspicion is the person who won it, Patrick Mackensie. Or a teacher.'

'We can't ask the House Matron,' I said, 'she's bound to start suspecting something.'

'No,' Sarah said, 'look how sparkling they are, the cleaner must have a key otherwise they'd be all dusty.'

'The groundsmen's room, that's what the cleaners use as their restroom, quick.'

We walked as quickly as could pushing Mason to the central court where pupils were sitting on the lawns in the four quadrants, beneath tall Oak trees in each, and followed the outside path around to an old door embedded in the wall and knocked.

An old lady came to the door with a cigarette dangling from her mouth. 'What is it, I'm having my tea, dears.'

'Do you know the boy that went missing, Patrick Mackensie?' Mason asked.

'I've already spoken to the police. I don't know anything about him, sorry, I can't help,' and started to close the door.

'Wait. Please, miss. We're making a card for his parents and we just wanted to take a picture of the trophy he won to put on the cover. Can you open the trophy cabinet for us, it will just take a second, and it would mean the world to them.'

'I've been on my feet all morning.'

'We'd be ever so grateful.'

She groaned and complained all the way back to the trophy cabinet like she didn't have the opportunity to talk much, carrying her large set of keys.

'I never get a moment's peace. If it's not one thing, it's another. Child sick in the toilets this morning, assembly at the last minute the other day, the entire floor needs to be swept. Polish the trophies. I've only got one pair of hands.'

We finally made it to the trophy cabinet and she searched her stack of keys and singled out a small thin brass one and opened the cabinet.

'Which one is it?'

We all pointed to the headmaster's trophy and she lifted it down for us.

Mason held it and I stood behind him as Sarah took the photo. And then Mason whispered out of the corner of his mouth, 'cover me.' I stepped in front of Mason. 'Come here, Sarah, show me the photo.' Shielded by our bodies, Mason lifted the lid of the cup, pulled something out, and put the lid back on. 'It's perfect, thank you so much Miss.'

She took the trophy off Mason, 'mind your grubby fingers, I've just polished that.' She placed it back on the centre shelf in pride of position and locked the cabinet. 'I hope it's worth it.'

'I'm sure his parents will be thrilled,' I said, grinning from ear-to-ear, 'thank you so much.'

'Now can I finish my tea?' She walked off talking to herself. 'I bet it's cold by now.'

'We should get her some flowers,' Sarah said, 'I bet she never gets any appreciation.'

'Did you find it?' I asked Mason. I wasn't as compassionate as Sarah, and hungry.

Mason waited for a teacher and two prefects to pass, and then held up a little ball, smiling, like holding a lottery ball with the winning number, 'Easy when you know how.'

'Give me it!' Sarah snatched the ball from his hand, unwrapped the message and popped the Malteser in her mouth. I couldn't believe it. I was speechless. Stunned watching her munch, like a dog watching his owner eat his supper. So much for compassion.

'Veni, vidi, vici, and there's another squiggle,' she chewed.

'Who cares about the squiggles. You ate my Malteser.' I said dejectedly.

'Grow up, Alex. It could be an O, or a U, but I think it's an A ... E.R.G.A.? Does that mean anything in Latin?'

'It's a preposition, towards,' Mason said, 'but it's got to be ten letters.'

'Maybe it's not one word, but two words,' I said, 'towards as in towards wherever he is?'

'What does the message say, give it back to me,' Mason said.

Mason read the message, torn again from a Latin dictionary, and said, 'everyone knows this one, Sarah: Not v*eni, vidi, vici*, the Romans pronounced the V like a W, 'Weni, Widi, Wici: I saw, I came, I conquered.'

'He's talking about the headmaster's trophy,' I said, 'he saw the prize, he rose to the challenge, and he won it.'

'And that was his downfall,' Mason slipped the torn paper in his inside blazer pocket, 'we've got to go, we'll be late for class.'

'This was so much easier when we didn't have to go to lessons,' I said to Sarah.

'What was the next song? We can do this quicker if we use lesson time like we did in music.'

'World's Smallest Violin by AJR'

If we didn't find him soon, I thought, the headmaster's trophy would be the only thing the school had to remember him by.

CHAPTER NINETEEN

The world's smallest violin

'Let's listen to it on the way to class. Give us your phone Mason,' Sarah said and handed me an earpiece and the World's Smallest Violin started to play.

Immediately I started to feel better with the light cheery thumb-snapping beat as we walked to P.S.E. (Personal and Social Education) and I suddenly didn't feel like finding Mason was a lost cause. Maybe that's how Patrick Mackensie felt when he left, I thought. He wasn't sad, he was happy to be putting his plan into action. He knew what he was doing. Look at all the messages, he must have been planning this for ages, and the moment he actually did it, must have been exciting.

'This is easy.' I said to Mason, 'it's a violin, of course. It's hollow. Miss Cathlewaite has violins in the cupboard. We just need to find the smallest one!'

'How are you going to get a Malteser through the f hole?' Sarah asked. 'Never mind, the smallest one.'

I scratched my chin; she had a point.

'What about the grand piano?' She said.

'You're both wrong. You're not listening to the lyrics. He sings he couldn't even finish school and bored his therapist playing the violin. When you play someone like a violin, you're manipulating their emotions. This is about counselling, trust me, I know. If Patrick Mackensie had counselling, it's got to be the counselling room.'

'I remember you saying Miss Proctor had a box of Maltesers in the cupboard. I haven't forgotten that—How could I! And now I remember, there were loads of empty packets of Maltesers in his drawer, and he's leaving a Malteser with every clue!'

'She always gives a packet of Maltesers after the session, she has nothing else. Maybe the Maltesers are a symbol of counselling or joining the dots.'

'That's very clever, Mason,' Sarah said, 'but it doesn't prove he had counselling. It could just be a coincidence.'

'I said *if* he had counselling. We can ask Miss Proctor.'

'What do you mean we?' I said.

'I told her I had a new roommate. She wants to meet you.'

'I'm not going to Miss Proctor,' Sarah said, 'people will think I'm crazy.'

'That's so rude, Sarah,' I said, 'Mason's not crazy. Take it back.'

'I'm sorry, I didn't mean you, Mason.'

'It doesn't matter, I'm used to it,' he said, reaching the PSE room just before Miss Gambol was about to start. Either nothing fazed him, or everything did.

We took our seats and I looked up at the whiteboard and read the title, 'Depression,' which was pretty depressing for a start.

'Last week we talked about how to identify our feelings,' Miss Gambol said, 'and this week, I want to talk to you about mental wellbeing.

'Our mental health is no different to our physical health. It's nothing to be embarrassed about. We can be physically fit and then we have an accident, like Mason on the rugby field, and we need to get better. We can be mentally fit and something happens and we similarly need to get better.

'Physical fitness is on a scale from very fit to very unfit, and it's the same with mental wellbeing; it's on a scale from very well mentally to very unwell mentally. It's perfectly normal; nobody's crazy.'

I shot Sarah a stare and she looked down guiltily.

'We're all somewhere on the scale and it can vary from time to time, regardless of how physically fit or worldly successful you are. In fact, you are more likely to suffer from depression if you are exceptionally intelligent or successful. It doesn't mean you are a loser in life, quite the reverse. Many geniuses have suffered from depression. Can anyone think of one ... Sarah?'

'Mozart, miss.'

'That's right, well done, Sarah. George?'

'Harry Kane.'

The class laughed.

'I'm not sure he's a genius, but why not.'

'I'm serious, miss. He was in a documentary with Prince William. He set up the Harry Kane Foundation to raise awareness about mental health.'

'Did he really? There you go, then. The England Captain. Anyone else?'

The only person I could think of was Mason, remembering what he was like the days after the accident, and I wondered if that was depression, too. But after the lesson, I didn't mention it as we walked to the counselling room.

'If he was having counselling,' I said, 'where would it be in the counselling room?'

'Where is a Malteser least likely to be noticed?'

'In a box of Maltesers?'

'Exactly.'

'Mason? You know, Sarah didn't really mean anything by it. I don't think you're crazy. Like Miss Gambol said, it's perfectly normal.'

'I don't want to talk about it, Alex. I have to do enough talking about it with Miss Proctor every Wednesday afternoon.'

'What's she like?'

He rolled his eyes, 'you'll see.'

We passed the Deputy Head's office next-door, and stopped outside a door with a sign printed, 'Dr Hilary Proctor.'

Mason knocked on the door and after a few moments it opened.

I looked up at a tall lady with long wild brown hair falling over a woollen jumper, and a string of beads around her neck like a hippy, and a long flowery dress to her ankles. She leaned her head to her side and slightly forward, 'Mason, how nice to see you,' holding her hand out to shake his hand. 'And you must be, Alex, his roommate, am I right? I'm Hilary.' She shook my hand like a long-lost friend with a big fake smile. 'Do come in.'

Instead of an office it was like a lounge with soft comfy armchairs in front of the open lit fire place and a long desk under the window with her laptop. I immediately noticed the metal filing cabinet in the corner.

'Do sit down and make yourselves comfortable.' She narrowed her eyes and leaned forward giving Mason her full attention like a car with its headlamps on full. 'How have you been *feeling*?'

'I'm fine. You said you wanted to meet Alex, so I thought we'd just stop by for a minute on our way to lunch.'

'Yes, I do, I do.' She turned her attention on me, and I almost physically jerked back. 'How are you finding Mason as a roommate? You must have got to really know one another sharing the same room.'

'He's great.'

'Great. You said great,' like she was listening to something underneath the words I said and just out of earshot, 'yes, I suppose he is great. Are you great, too, Alex?'

Was she this intense with everybody, I thought, but I didn't know how she expected me to answer so I just shrugged, 'I do my best.'

'But you think Mason is better?'

I raised my eyebrows like I'd been trapped in a corner. Was she trying to counsel me too, perhaps she couldn't help herself, like a policeman trained to distrust.

'We're like a team, miss.'

'Don't call me, miss,' she laughed, 'I'm not a teacher, call me Hilary. We're perfectly equal in here, aren't we Mason?'

Mason looked out of the corner of his eye at me and nodded, 'Hilary, can I ask you something?'

Her whole body swung on the edge of her seat to face him. 'Yes, of course, Mason. You know you can ask me anything.'

'When the headmaster mentioned Patrick Mackensie in assembly, I was wondering if he had any counselling?'

'You know I can't discuss a client. Everything's confidential between these four walls. Just as I can't discuss anything you tell me in confidence, unless it would cause harm to someone else or yourself, I'm sorry.'

'But you told the Police.'

'Yes, if it puts your mind at ease, I spoke to the Police. But, like I said, I can't discuss a client. Was there anything else?'

'Yes, Hilary. I had an episode and I missed lessons on Tuesday morning, can you write me a note for my teachers, please?'

'Is that all? Of course, I can,' she jumped up and sat at her laptop, and read out as she typed, 'To whom it may concern, please forgive Mason's absence in lessons due to treatment he is receiving under my care. Is that alright? Good. Print. I'll just pop to the admin office to get a hard copy, and stamp it for you. I'll be right back.'

After she closed the door, I said, 'Wow.'

'She does all it all the time. That's why I don't care about missing any lessons. Now, quick, the Maltesers are in the bottom drawer of that filing cabinet.'

I pulled out the drawer, it wasn't even locked to my surprise, and behind the vertical suspension files, was a large box emblazoned Maltesers with red packets all over it.

Inside I've never seen so many packets of Maltesers in my life. If this was what being a psychologist was like, sign me up. I dug my hand through the packets and felt around the bottom of the box because I couldn't see what I was doing without taking them all out. I suddenly felt a small lump, 'I've got it!'

'Keep your voice down.'

I pulled it out, quickly put it in my pocket, closed the draw and just as I sat down, the door opened.

'Sorry to keep you waiting.' She went to her desk and stamped the sheet of paper and handed it to Mason.

'Any problems ask them to call me, but I'm sure it will be fine.'

'Thank you so much, Hilary.'

'Now let's see if I have a little something for you both for taking the time to visit me.'

She opened the same drawer I had just been in and handed us a packet of Maltesers each. I felt a bit guilty accepting it, after what I'd just done, but the joy of anticipation quickly overcame that as we left the room.

Outside, I high-fived Mason, which must have seemed weird outside the counsellor's office to pupils walking by, but I didn't care if they thought we were crazy. We had the fifth message; we were half-way there; the end was in sight; we were definitely going to find Patrick Mackensie now.

'Let's wait to open it with Sarah, she'll be so excited.' I wanted to impress her.

'What these?' He held up his packet.

'Are you crazy?' I tore my packet open and filled my mouth with a handful, like the heavens raining cash after days of being drip-fed erratic pocket money. To a connoisseur like me, I must say, they were even better fresh.

'Fine, let's find her in the canteen. You can eat while you push. Come on, I want to find out what the message is.'

'This is the last time I am pushing you.'

I reluctantly put the packet in my blazer pocket and started pushing his wheelchair. The sooner he was out of this confounded wheelchair the better; chocolate is important to my mental wellbeing.

CHAPTER TWENTY

Toilet trouble

S arah smiled when we arrived at her table in the packed canteen
with a queue a mile long to get food.

'What was Miss Proctor like?'

'You mean Hilary?' I said taking a seat beside her.

'Are you on first name terms? She must like you.'

'She has her advantages,' Mason waved the permission letter,
although she wasn't asking him, 'it's my get-out-jail-free card.
Works every time.'

I showed her my packet of Maltesers. 'I think I need counselling,
too. Free Maltesers!' And continued where I had left off, popping
one in my mouth, 'Just don't say Mason's great,' she looked at me
quizzically, 'it's a long story.'

'Did Patrick Mackensie have counselling?'

'She said she couldn't discuss a *client*, but had talked to the Police
about him. You can't get a clearer confirmation than that.'

'Don't keep me in suspense, did you find it or not?'

I reached into my pocket and handed her the small lump under the table. She unwrapped the paper and ate the Malteser inside. I didn't mind, I already had a packet.

'There's another squiggle. It could be an S ... E.R.G.A.S., ergas?'

'It doesn't mean anything in Latin,' Mason said.

'I told you, the S must be the start of a new word. Erga, towards, towards the location, something beginning with S. We need to find the other clues.'

'Give it to me,' Mason said.

She covered it with her palm and slid her hand across the table and Mason looked down the table to make sure nobody was looking at them, and read it under the table, 'si vis pacem, para bellum: *if you want peace, prepare for war.*'

'Do you think he was fed up of counselling?' I said, 'I would be.'

'No. It's not *that* bad. She was just testing you. He's talking about the escape.'

'This is so weird,' Sarah said, looking at her half-finished salad and placed her knife and fork in the five-o-clock position. 'I don't feel like eating. It's like he's talking to us.'

'That's how I felt,' I said, 'it's eerie, isn't it.'

'Maybe we should go to the police,' she said, 'I don't feel comfortable anymore.'

'They're just torn scraps of paper from a Latin dictionary,' Mason said, 'the police would laugh at us. We can't stop now.'

'We all know it's more than that. The police can't be that stupid.'

Mason raised his eyebrows above the patch, 'Really? Then why haven't they found him. It's been almost a week. Patrick Mackensie needs us. He could be in danger. We don't know where he is if we don't follow the clues.'

Sarah sighed deeply, 'Hurry up then. What's the next song?'

'I'm Not Famous by AJR,' I said, 'give us your phone, Mason.'

I shared the earpiece with her, and at the glockenspiel reply, almost in spite of herself, she looked at me and smiled, and we both nodded our heads in time to the cheery music, while Mason rolled his eyes and looked at his watch.

'Well?' Mason asked when we stopped nodding our heads, 'which room?'

'He doesn't want people to hate him,' I said.

'No,' Sarah said, 'he wants to disappear so nobody will hate him. He doesn't want to be famous. He doesn't want to be known as the winner of the headmaster's prize anymore.'

'But which room?' Mason hissed under his breath.

The bell rang.

'We've got to go to Maths,' Sarah said.

'I've got to see the Medic. Alex, can you push me?'

'No, I told you that was the last time. You can walk. You can push the chair yourself.'

'Fine,' Mason said sorely, 'Try and think of the room, I'll wheel myself.' He rolled off in a huff.

Sarah and I stood and walked to class.

'Sometimes I think he likes being an invalid,' I said, 'I think he'll miss it.'

Sarah laughed.

Mr Thornton stood at the front of the class like a giant haystack with shoulder length hair, a long beard and a belly that bulged over the front of his trousers. We were all scared of him.

Everyone knew of the African artifacts in his adjoining office, like the curved antique dagger in the locked glass cabinet on his desk. I'm sure he kept it on display to scare pupils.

'Today, we're going to solve for X. X is what we don't know. We need to rearrange the equation until we have the unknown value on its own on one side of the equal sign ...'

I wrote in the back of my book, and nudged Sarah beside me, 'X=Room.'

'And then all the known values on the other side of the equal sign, and then you'll know just what the unknown value is.'

She wrote back, 'what are the known values?'

I scribbled, 'art, Latin, pop music.'

'But how do we that?' Mr Thornton said, 'How do we rearrange the known facts. We know that Algebra uses the four main operations, addition, subtraction, multiplication and division ...'

She wrote, 'rearrange them.'

I wrote, 'Latin, pop music, art,' and then shook my head and put a line through them, 'Latin, pop music, art,' looking at her gravely, and wrote, 'Boy's dorm room. Left clothes. School bag. Where isn't he known? Where can't he go?'

'The girl's dorm,' she wrote and smiled at me, 'especially not naked!'

'And then we can use the operations to rearrange the equation as long as we understand one really important thing first. We need to understand that an equation is like a balance scale.'

I wrote, 'too many rooms.' And then I had a brilliant idea, and wrote, 'girls' toilets! Definitely not known there.'

'I hope not!' she wrote, 'but too many.'

'If there's the same amount of weight on both sides then the scales are in balance. It's like in ancient African culture ...' I thought about the dagger in his office when he said that. I'm sure every pupil did.

'Where's only one female toilet?' I whispered in her ear.

'Miss Haversham in the art block!' She whispered back.

'But if we add weight to just one side then the scales will tip. The two sides are no longer in balance. That is the African secret to life and algebra.'

'She's his art teacher,' I whispered.

We both looked at each other and I could see admiration and esteem in her eyes. For the first time, I thought, she really did fancy me. The feeling was mutual. She has such beautiful eyes; brown, like maltesers. I tried to concentrate on the worksheet Mr Thornton told us to do online, but it was hard with her sitting next to me, and the butterflies in my stomach.

After the lesson, it was a shock to see Mason standing outside without a wheelchair in sight. He suddenly seemed taller although he was still only five-foot; like Mozart, I thought.

'You two look like you have something to tell me.'

'We solved for X,' I said, 'Miss Haversham's toilet! We've got her next. I'll explain on the way.'

Mason limped after us, but at least he could walk.

Miss Haversham had grey hair, severe dark eyebrows and was plump. She didn't tolerate fools lightly. If there wasn't absolute silence in the room, or anyone spoke while they were supposed to be drawing, she'd stop the music, which played soothingly in the background, and spout behaviour points like a sub-machine gun.

Today she gently asked us to draw a bowl of fruit she'd placed at the centre of each group of four large art tables. She went around the room observing us and commenting.

Half-way through the lesson, and I'm not sure whether that was intentionally timed by Mason, because she usually asked pupils to wait if they needed the bathroom, which was ironic considering she had her own and never needed to, Mason raised his hand.

'I'm desperate for the restroom Miss, but I don't have my wheelchair. It will take me all lesson to limp to the toilets and back. I have a note.'

'Can't you see I'm in the middle of something. Why didn't you go before the lesson?'

'I didn't have time, miss. The doctor was examining my ankle.'

'This is the exception that proves the rule,' she held up her key, and made him hobble over to her to collect it, 'bring it straight back.'

He went in to the toilet and I held my breath counting the seconds until he opened the door with a big smile. I noticed the edge of his right shirt cuff was wet.

'What are you smiling for?' Miss Haversham noticed him.

'Relief.'

The class laughed.

'Everyone back to work. And never ask me again, Mason, wheelchair or no wheelchair.'

'Thank you, miss,' Mason looked down glumly and then looked up at me and smiled. I knew he had found it.

CHAPTER TWENTY-ONE

Death and destruction

Mason refused to show us the package until we got him back to our dorm room. I think he just wanted the company, or to bask in the glow of Sarah's unadulterated attention as long as possible.

I closed the room door behind us.

'Da-dah!' Mason collapsed on the bed and held up a shining silver little ball, it had tin foil wrapped around it.

'Where was it?' Sarah said.

'Oh no, not the bowl?' I grimaced at the thought, 'your sleeve is wet.'

'The cistern. I rolled my sleeve up but it was right at the bottom near the outlet pipe. I had to stand on the bowl to reach it and almost lost my balance and fell in. Can you imagine Miss Haversham's face if I walked out with a wet shoe?'

Sarah and I laughed.

'That would have been hysterical,' I said, 'especially when you said 'relief'.'

We all laughed.

'Open it,' Sarah said excitedly.

'But the Malteser's mine,' I said territorially.

'Actually, I'm not sure I want to know after the last one, 'Sarah said, 'this is scary.'

Mason carefully undid the foil, picking at it with his fingernails, and then unwrapped the torn message and threw me the Malteser. I tried to catch it in my mouth, but missed, and picked it off the floor, shrugged, and ate it anyway.

'Is there a squiggle?' Sarah asked.

'I think it's a T. But what's this?'

'E.R.G.A.S.T., ergast, does it mean anything in Latin?' Sarah asked.

'No,' he said, 'but this is strange ...'

'Is nobody listening to me? I told you it's the start of a new word,' I said, 'think about words beginning S.T. with four more letters ...'

'Carthago delenda est. *Carthage must be destroyed.*'

'Who on earth is Carthage?' Sarah said worryingly.

'It used to be a place in Northern Africa. Carthage was the most powerful ancient Phoenician city in Roman times. A politician, I can't remember his name, would end all his speeches to the senate with this line before they went to war.'

'Why does Patrick Mackensie hate an ancient city?' I said, 'it doesn't make any sense.'

'It's not literal. It's an expression which means absolute support for an idea. Carthago delenda est. It led to the devastating death and destruction of Carthage by the Roman army and history has never forgiven them.'

'Do you think he wants to destroy the school,' I said, 'or its reputation?'

'This is heavy,' Sarah said. 'I think Patrick Mackensie is ... very troubled. But that's perfectly normal.'

'Could be,' he said, 'it depends on what he said in the next message.'

'What is the next song?' Sarah asked. 'We've got to do it now. We can't wait until tomorrow. The whole school could be at risk.'

I found it in my journal. 'I don't believe it. It's by AJR, too, it's called *Bang*.'

'Oh my goodness, not a bomb?' Sarah's eyes opened wide.

'Keep your voice down, Sarah,' Mason said.

There was a knock at the door and we all turned to look at it.

The House Matron popped her head around the door without waiting for an answer. Had she been listening behind it? She had a pile of envelopes in her hand and waved one in the air at me.

'You've got mail, Alex. What are you doing in the boys' dorm, Sarah?'

'Carrying Mason's books,' she said, I was just leaving.' And left.

'That's very kind of Sarah. I should give her a house point. Don't forget to remind your parents it's the Parent Teacher's Evening next Friday. Have a lovely evening.' She closed the door behind her.

I had been pushing Mason around for a week, and she hadn't given me a single house point.

I immediately recognised the handwriting on the envelope. 'It's from my father. But why would he write if I'm seeing him on Friday?'

'Perhaps he can't make it. My parents are not coming. I wonder if Patrick Mackensie's parents will?'

I read the letter and began to cry.

CHAPTER TWENTY-TWO

Bad news

'Dear Alex,' my father wrote, 'I hope everything is going well for you at school. I'm sorry to have to tell you, your mother and I have decided to live apart for a while.

'It isn't because of anything you've done. This has been on the cards for a very long time, but I stayed because I love you.

'I've always tried to do my best for you, but your mother has her opinions and I have mine. She misses you more than earth itself and I'm too tired to argue anymore.

'The good news is you'll be going to Fishdown Comprehensive next term with all your old friends, which I know is what you really wanted.

'Forgive me for not listening to you, I was only thinking about your future, and I just wanted you to have a better life than mine.

'I'll be staying with grandma and grandpa and Mama agreed you can stay with us for a week before Christmas. You can call me on your mobile, or whatever you used before, if you want to talk.

'I love you, Papa.'

It was like my whole world collapsing as the tears rolled down my face. I felt angry and upset all at the same time. Why he couldn't he tell me to my face? Why did it have to be a letter? I hated him.

'What's wrong, Alex?' Mason asked gently.

'What's it got to do with you?' I said and stormed out of the room. I ran down the corridor, tears streaming down my face, round and round the descending staircase to the ground floor, and out of the building. I didn't know where I was running to.

I ran past the sports fields, through the horse riding fields and into the woods, the leaves crunching under my feet, dodging the trees that stood in my way. I heaved for breath and started walking and finally sat down on a fallen tree.

It wasn't fair, I thought, why me? Why can't I be like everyone else and have a normal life and normal parents. Why did my father have to be a drunk and go to prison? Why did he have to leave my mum? How would we survive without my father? She was *only*, as my father always said, a waitress. How could I start a new school now? How could I find Patrick Mackensie if I wasn't even at the Grange. I couldn't see any solution whichever way I looked, information overload, too much to comprehend. How could he do this to me if he loved me?

It wasn't fair, it just wasn't fair. I cried and cried and cried until there were no tears left in me and I was totally spent and exhausted.

I thought about running away but I didn't even have my school bag with me. That's it, I thought. I had to go back and plan my escape, just like Patrick Mackensie. Go somewhere they would never find me.

It was beginning to get dark, and shadows began to form around me as the sunset disappeared. I forced myself to get up but I didn't know which way I'd come.

I heard voices, a low rumbling, like chanting, coming from behind me, deep in the woods. I thought I must be hallucinating or something.

I walked towards the noise to prove it wasn't just my imagination and I wasn't losing my mind, and it grew louder. I stepped through brambles and a thorn pierced my leg, which stung, but I kept on walking, until I saw the flickering orange light of fire between the trees.

As I got closer, I could see burning torches being held aloft by people chanting in a circle around a big fire at the centre, dressed in costumes like nomadic desert tribes with ornate headdresses that masked their eyes and long flowing robes with gold ropes tied around their waist, carrying long curved daggers on their hip that glinted in the firelight.

I counted ten of them, and judging from their lips, the outlines of bosoms and their footwear—they were oddly wearing normal shoes—five of them were women.

I tried to make out what they were saying, but it was in another language, and I was distracted by the overpowering smell of pork and incense.

I stepped closer, as silently as possibly, and saw a piglet staring at me from the fire like it was being roasted alive, flames rising around its head and little pointy ears.

I panicked and stepped on a branch which snapped and one of the largest ghost-like figures spun around and pulled off their headdress, putting their hand above their eyes to shield them from the light of the fire, and see into the darkness. He had long grey hair and a long beard and I recognised him immediately. It was Mr, Thornton, our Maths teacher, staring straight at me.

I was so surprised I stepped back and fell over backwards, twisting my ankle on a root. I looked up and he was coming towards me. I scrambled to my feet and ran as fast as I could hoping he hadn't seen my face, panting and urging myself not to stop, scared to look back in case he was gaining on me.

When I couldn't run another step, I looked back, and there was nobody there.

I leaned on my knees trying to catch my breath and not vomit, but I couldn't hold it back, and threw up on the spot, just missing my school shoes. There was a vile taste in my mouth, behind the front teeth, and I tried to swallow it down, but it didn't go away.

I marched on until I finally saw the lights in the windows of the dorms twinkling like a doll's house in the distance. There was nobody about, just the sound of an owl hooting far away, and a lorry coming, as I ploughed through the muddy fields, relieved to be out of the woods in the open air, and looked up at the stars filling the sky and the lonely moon.

As I neared the North Tower, I could see the lorry was a coal truck, parked alongside, with its engine still running, lights on and indicators flashing with a wide yellow chute running into the side of the building and a man operating a panel at the back. I gave him a wide berth so as not to be seen, but I tripped on the step coming into the building and when I looked back, he was looking straight at me.

I finally reached my dorm room, too tired to think when Mason asked me, 'Where have you been? I thought you'd done a Patrick Mackensie and left for good.'

'There's something going on in the woods,' I undid my muddy shoe laces, 'I don't know if it has anything to do with Patrick Mackensie's disappearance, but I saw them roasting a piglet alive. They were wearing headdresses which covered their eyes, but I could see their lips. Five men and five women, I think.'

'A sacrifice?'

'I don't know what it was, but it was staring into my eyes with its head in flames,' I winced at the memory and felt sick again, 'they were chanting in something like Latin.'

'What were they saying, I'll try and translate.'

'I don't know,' I lay down on my bed, 'look, Mason, it's been a long day. Can we talk about this in the morning, please?'

'You can't just tell me that and go to sleep. A boy's life is at stake.'

I put the pillow over my head, 'Goodnight Mason.'

I fell asleep thinking about my mum.

CHAPTER TWENTY-THREE

The Bang!

In the morning, the room looked exactly the same, but the world felt different, like it had turned on its axis and started going a different way, and all the old laws of Physics no longer applied.

I had always taken it for granted that my parents would be together forever, it's not something I ever questioned, even in their most ferocious arguments, but I didn't want to discuss it with Mason. Some things are best kept private, like he always said. It was a good thing he wanted to know everything about the gathering in the woods, it kept my mind off it.

'This changes everything,' he said, 'by the way, your shoes are ruined.'

'My whole life is ruined,' I said without thinking, before I could retract it, and I told him about the letter.

'You should talk to Miss Proctor.'

'I thought you said never to talk anybody.'

'Not about your *feelings*. You can tell anyone about your feelings, they're not facts, but they feel like them sometimes, especially if you don't. She said we make stories in our head to try and protect ourselves, but who knows if they're right or wrong unless you discuss them with someone. She can't tell anyone else. Everything you say is confidential, unless you want to hurt yourself or someone else.'

'I don't know. I don't know if I can trust her. What if she tells my teachers?'

'She's sworn an oath of secrecy. She can't. Trust me, I trust her. Like miss said, we all are less mentally well sometimes, like me injuring my ankle. It's perfectly normal.'

I did feel confused but I was scared of talking to Miss Proctor, 'I don't know.'

'I bet your father has been to a counsellor. My parents certainly have. My father says it costs him a fortune for my mother. They have to pay in America.'

'I haven't got any money.'

'It's free. Just go in and show her the letter and she'll give you a bag of Maltesers. It's easy if you're honest.'

I said I'd think about it, but thinking about the bag of Maltesers decided, 'I'll go at break, but don't tell Sarah.'

'I'm sure she'd ... OK, OK, I promise.'

There was a knock at the door, and it opened slightly, 'Are you decent?'

'Speak of the devil,' Mason said.

'Have you started without me? What did the House Matron say?'

'She's going to give you a house point for carrying my books,' he said, 'thanks for that. I hadn't even noticed.'

'Yes, funny how she gives *girls* house points for helping Mason,' I said, 'but I suppose that's not sexist.'

Sarah giggled, 'I'll give you the next Malteser, I promise. But what about the bomb? I mean the Bang! Have you figured it out, yet?'

'Events have overtaken us.' Mason said. 'This might be far bigger than I thought it was.'

'Bigger than a bomb?' Sarah said incredulously.

I told her about the gathering in the woods.

'What were you doing in the middle of the woods at night?'

'It's a long story, but I recognised one of the gatherers.'

'Don't tell me, the headmaster?'

'Mr Thornton, he was wearing a long dress and carrying a curved dagger.'

'The Maths teacher? What were they doing?'

'Sacrificing a pig,' Mason said, 'it must be a ritual of some kind. Alex said they were chanting.'

'It wasn't a pig. It was a piglet. They were burning it alive. I saw it with my own eyes.'

Sarah squeezed her eyes shut, 'That's so cruel, I don't want to picture it. It sounds like the Lord of the Flies. Carry on.'

'That was it. He tried to catch me but I got away. I don't know what it's got to do with Patrick Mackensie. But Mason thinks ...'

'I think it has to be related. A secret society and the secret disappearance of a missing boy. It's too strange to be merely a coincidence.'

'How do you know it's a secret society?' She asked.

'Why are they wearing masks, chanting in long robes in the woods in the middle of the night and burning a piglet alive. It's not exactly a typical staff meeting.'

'We've got to go to the police,' she said.

'What if the police are involved?' Mason said, 'we don't know who was there besides Mr Thornton, but if a teacher is there, it could be anyone in authority.'

'This is heavy,' she said.

'You think this is bad, you try being there. I was petrified.'

'Play the next song, it might be a clue,' she said, 'maybe Patrick Mackensie will give us a message about them if it is related.'

Mason pressed play on his laptop and left to go to the bathroom.

Sarah mimed the opening piano notes of Bang with her fingers while I clicked my fingers and swayed to the gentle beat. She stood up and took my hand and raised it putting her other arm around my waist and I copied her, like a proper couple's dance, stepping side to side and gently swaying, until both her arms were around me, and mine hers, and we rested our heads on each other's shoulders, still swaying and stepping side-to-side. It was such a relief to feel her living, breathing body so close to mine, I could have cried. Just Sarah and I, two lonely kids who had found a moment of peace in all the turmoil, together.

It was like a farewell dance, I thought, only she didn't know it yet.

We heard the door open and Sarah and I quickly stepped apart and looked around the room conspicuously, making it obvious that something had just happened, as Mason limped in.

'Have you figured out the room?' he said.

I hadn't been listening to a word of the song, my mind had been somewhere else, and looked at Sarah helplessly.

'He sings go out with a bang,' she said, 'which means stop existing or doing something in an exciting way.'

Mason shook his head, 'You weren't listening. He sings he got a flat opposite the park and left quinoa in the fridge in the first verse. I didn't need to hear the rest. Where is the only flat opposite a park with a fridge, here? The Sports pavilion opposite the playing fields. They got me an icepack from the fridge when I injured my ankle. There's no reference to any other place in the song, it has to be it. We've got Games, now, but I'm excused, remember. Come on, let's go.'

'I've got Hockey,' Sarah said, 'I'll see you later, Alex.'

'Sure,' I said.

CHAPTER TWENTY-FOUR

Betrayal

I changed into my rugby gear quickly and followed Mason to the small kitchenette in the Pavilion, while the other boys finished dressing.

We checked the coast was clear. Mr Swanson made his coffee here, but I could see him waiting outside for the boys to line up, talking to Mr Thornton, who looked more ridiculous with a whistle around his neck in a tracksuit, with his big belly hanging over the bottoms, than dressed in his long robes.

Mason opened the counter-high small fridge, and it was practically empty, save for three cartons of milk.

'Try the freezer box.'

Mason lifted the flap, and I saw two icepacks. He pulled them out, and behind them, embedded in the white ice which made it difficult to see if you weren't looking for it, I could just make out a small white lump.

'It won't budge,' Mason said, his face reddening with the strain of pulling it.

I opened the cutlery drawer and handed him a table spoon, 'Here, use this.'

He held it like a dagger and chopped away at the ice until he finally freed it.

'What's going on here?' Mr Swanson suddenly boomed over my shoulder.

I spun around, 'We were just getting an icepack for Mason's ankle, sir.'

'Did the doctor tell you to get an icepack?'

'No, but it still feels sore,' Mason winced in pain.

'If the doctor didn't say use an icepack,' he picked them off the counter, and put them back, 'you don't use an icepack. If it's still sore you see the doctor, is that clear? Ask for painkillers, you don't go in my fridge.'

'It won't happen again, sir. Sorry, sir.'

'Next time it's a behaviour point. Alex, go with Mason to the sickbay.'

We left but we didn't go to the sickbay and instead went straight back to our dorm room.

Mason unwrapped the paper around the lump carefully but it ripped in two. 'It's OK,' he said, 'I can still read it.'

He tossed me the Malteser and I put it in my mouth without thinking. It was as hard as a marble, and spit it out into my hand. 'This is rock solid. I really have to get a fresh packet from Miss Proctor, now. What does it say?'

'There's another squiggle.'

'It's a shame Sarah's not here. She would love that. Shouldn't we wait for her?'

'There isn't time. It looks like a U.'

'E.R.G.A. ... Towards, S.T.U. ... Six letters? Let me get my dictionary.'

I flicked through the pages to the S's, and ran my finger down the page until I came to the STU's and counted the letters, and wrote them in my journal, calling each one out, 'Studeo (To search), Stulte, Stulti, Stulto (Fool), Stupeō (Stunned), Stupor (Numb), Stuppa (Tow), Stupri, (Dishonour or sex?). I think that's all of them, but it narrows it down. The only one that sounds like a room, is Stupor, *numb*. Could it be the sickbay?'

'Do you really think he's hiding in the sickbay? How many times have we been there. Where, exactly, under the hospital bed? No. Listen to this, though ...'

'But there are no other six letter words in Latin beginning S.T.U. ...'

'*Et tu, Brute*? It means, *And you, Brutus*? It's from Shakespeare's play, Julius Caesar, he says it at the very moment of his assassination by Brutus. It's an expression which means betrayal, literally being stabbed in the back by a friend.'

'Who's Brutus? He didn't have any friends. We found it in the Pavilion, could it be Mr Swanson?'

'No, he hated sports. He was an artist.'

'Miss Haversham, his art teacher?'

'She isn't anybody's friend.'

'Miss Proctor, his counsellor?'

'That's what I thought at first, she's the only teacher on first-name terms with pupils, but he's already left a clue there.'

'I give up. What was the next song?'

'This Ain't a Scene, It's an Arms Race by Fall Out Boy.'

'Play it on your phone and give me an earpiece quick.'

A wow sound like a spaceship landing got louder, a guitar squealed like a cat being trod on, and a man cried like a tortured confession he was an arms dealer. The bass drum thumped like a rhino trotting, stabbing rhythm guitar in the background, base walking up and down stairs, muffled words echoed, until he cried, what sounded like, this ain't a city, it's a goddam arms race. The pace suddenly went hyper like a machine gun firing and he sung he was the leading man, weaving intricate lies, drums beating at what seemed like two hundred beats a minute. Over and over again, he sung he was the leading man, weaving intricate lies ...

'I don't get it,' I said, 'there isn't a teacher who's an arms dealer?'

'Who is the only teacher with a dagger?'

I suddenly pictured Mr Thornton in the woods and his long dagger.

'Mr *Thornton*!' We both said simultaneously.

'He's the leading man,' I said incredulously, 'it all makes sense. The leader of the secret society. And ... he must be telling lies.'

'But leading who?'

'We've got to get into his office,' I said, 'it must be in the display box with the dagger. But I can't go now; I've got to see Miss Proctor at break.'

'No problem. We have Maths third period. We'll do it then.'

'How?'

'I'll think of something, but when I do, just make sure you distract him, and he doesn't follow me into his office, OK?'

I nodded, but I still didn't know how he was going to get in there.

Chapter Twenty-Five

The million dollar question

I knocked on Miss Proctor's door nervously and she opened it, leaning her head to the side, 'Alex? How nice to see you. You're not with Mason?'

'No, miss, I mean Hilary. I wondered if I could talk to you privately about something.'

'Of course, you can,' and then said like an aside, 'that's what they pay me for. Do come in.'

I sat in the comfy armchair in front of the open fire as she shovelled more coals on and sat down. But after she asked me what she could do to help, I didn't know where to start, so I just handed her the letter from my father, like Mason had told me to.

Her eyes narrowed on it like reading an exam question.

'What should I do?'

'Ah, the million-dollar question. *What should I do*? That's not how this works, Alex. I can't give you the answer. But I can help you find your own. How does the letter make you feel?'

'Angry. But I know it's my fault, I shouldn't have called him. I said I didn't want to be here, but I do now. I was just homesick. And now they're going to split up because of me. My whole life is ruined but ...'

'They're going to split up because of you,' she said. Why was she repeating everything I said, I thought, when I already knew what I'd just said.

'Yes, it's obvious,' I said.

'It's obvious? I'm sorry, but can you hear yourself? What you're thinking? The assumptions you're making? You're telling yourself a story in your head, and mind-reading what other people are thinking. It's an autonomous dysfunctional belief. Have you ever seen your parents argue before?'

'All the time.'

'And what do they argue about?'

'Usually about money. He hasn't got a job. Or his drinking,' I looked down embarrassedly.

'Are you saying that they *usually* argue about money or his drinking?' I raised my eyebrows, was she going to repeat everything I said? She waited for me to continue.

'He has a fiery temper and is always calling her an effing c word and afterwards gives me 10p for each c word as if that makes it OK?'

'Do you think that makes it OK?'

'I don't know. No. Of course, not. But he can't stand it when she tells him to get a proper job.'

'Why do you think he can't stand it when she tells him to get a proper job?'

'Maybe because he's trying to be a writer but doesn't sell any books or can't get a proper job?'

'How do you think that makes him feel?'

'Powerless. Angry. I don't know. He pushed her once on the shoulder in the bedroom, the door was open and I saw her fall over. I was terrified but she got up and started screaming that he'd hit her and she was going to call the police and wanted a divorce.'

'How did that make you feel?'

'Angry … Powerless … The same … Scared? My father has never hit me, but if he can hit my mum or take her phone, I don't know.'

'And then what happened?'

'He locked her out and the police came and arrested him. He spent the night in jail and then he didn't talk to my mum except to call her an effing c word as usual. She said she was taking us back to Malaysia to live with grandma when she saves up enough money.'

'How does that make you feel?'

'I feel like I'm split in half, right down the middle. I don't want to go but I can't do anything.' I was starting to get flustered and my head was like a swarm of bees. It was hopeless. I didn't want to cry and fought back the urge.

'Is that your fault? That your father hasn't got a job, or no money, or his drinking, or calls your mum names or hits her or they don't speak or your mother wants to leave him?'

'No!' I began to cry in a fit of rage and self-disgust, 'but I made the call,' she waited without saying a word, 'I don't know what to do.'

'Parents pass their issues to their children like DNA,' she shook her head. 'Do you think it's wrong for a boy to call home when he feels homesick?'

'No, day by day I'm just putting on a brave face.' I stopped sniveling and she handed me a tissue, and I wiped my eyes and blew my nose, 'I don't want to go to Fishdown Comprehensive.'

'Oh, you don't want to go to Fishdown Comprehensive, really?'

I stopped for a moment. I didn't. She was right. 'But what can I do?'

'I don't know. What can you do if you want something from your parents?'

'Talk to them?' I said and she shrugged. 'Explain why I don't want to leave?' She shrugged again. 'Try and convince them?'

'It seems to me you have answered your own question.'

I looked up out of the tall window at a bird flying in the sky, and I felt lighter, too. And part of the heavy weight holding me down seemed to have lifted from my shoulders. She was right. Was it that simple? I just had to persuade my mother, and then maybe they wouldn't split up after all.

'Thank you, m ... Hilary.'

'I didn't do anything; you did all the work.'

It was funny her calling it work, it didn't seem like work, it was more like space to think.

Mason was right; it was easy, if you were honest.

Maybe that's where Patrick Mackensie went wrong; he kept too many secrets. And maybe I would make a good psychologist after all, whatever autonomous dysfunctional beliefs meant, I was determined to find out one day.

I couldn't believe she got paid for doing this; just sitting in a chair and repeating everything I said; It was the perfect job for me.

I watched her rifle in her bottom drawer and pull out a pack of Maltesers, like the icing on the cake.

'For the ultimate detective!' She handed them to me.

That remark was a bit too close to home, but I could see from her smile she didn't suspect anything.

I practically flew out the door to Maths class, gobbling chocolate.

I didn't want to be late.

There was a dagger waiting for us.

CHAPTER TWENTY-SIX

The assyrian sickle sword

I saw Mason sitting at the back of the Maths room and waved at him with a big smile, holding the edge of my Malteser packet from my blazer pocket and he gave me the thumbs up sign.

I took my seat beside Sarah and she smiled at me. I wanted to tell her that everything was going to be OK, but she wouldn't have known what I was talking about.

Mr Thornton took the register and started.

'In the last lesson we looked at basic algebraic operations, solving for X. Today we are looking at Polynomials. A polynomial is a combination of terms, like 2X or 2X squared, the two being the number and the X being the variable. Remember the multiplication is always implied without having to write the symbol or multiply sign, and the number always comes first. The variable can be to any power, if it doesn't have a power sign, it means the variable has a factor of one.

'The variable is power,' she wrote in the back of her exercise book.

'We've found the room,' I wrote and when she looked at me, I nodded ever so slightly at Mr Thornton's office and her pupils widened in surprise.

'If the variable is squared it has a factor of two, and so on, to the power of three, four, five or whatever. A poly, in Latin meaning many, and nomial, meaning name or term, polynomial is simply terms connected by operations, such as addition, subtraction, multiplication or division.'

Mason put his hand up. 'Were polynomials invented by the Egyptians, sir?'

The class laughed.

'I don't think this is a laughing matter. Be quiet! It's a very interesting question. Although polynomials were officially discovered by René Descartes in 1637, ancient Babylonians as far back as 2000-1900 BC, were using them.'

'How do you know, sir?' Charlie sniggered. 'Were you there?'

The class laughed again.

'That's a behaviour point. Actually, Charles, for your information, Plimpton 322 is a Babylonian clay tablet containing Pythagorean triples', and wrote on the whiteboard, calling aloud, 'A squared plus B squared equals C squared' and drew a triangle with A on the short side, a right angle to B on the long side and C on the diagonal hypotenuse. 'They used a slightly more complicated polynomial, and wrote the formula, 'C squared over

B squared equals one plus A squared over B squared. Over three thousand six hundred years *before* Descartes.'

Mason put his hand up again. 'Is it true you've got a Babylonian dagger, sir?'

'It's a replica of an Assyrian sickle sword, Mason,' he smiled, 'would you like to see it?'

Everyone in the class nodded and Mr Thornton rolled his eyes like he was used to the enthusiasm. 'I know, I know.' He took the key out of his pocket and while he opened the door, I looked at Mason mouthing 'NOW, NOW, NOW' at me like an owl gone crazy, but I didn't know how I was supposed to distract Mr Thornton when he came out carrying the long curved gleaming silver sword I recognised immediately as the one he'd been wearing at the ritual. I could see the glass case with its lid hanging open on his desk in the office and realised this was our only chance.

'The Assyrian king used to carry this as a symbol of royal power. If you look closely ...'

'Sir, sir,' I waved my hand in the air.

'What is it, Alex?'

'Can I go to the toilet, sir? I've got diarrhoea!'

The class laughed.

'You'd better hurry, then.'

'... You can see an engraving of an antelope, and the inscription which appears in three places, on both sides of the blade and on the blunt side, 'Palace of Adad-nirari, king of the universe, son of Arik-den-ili, king of Assyria, son of Enlil-nirari, king of Assyria.'

I stopped outside the classroom panicking, what now, how can I get Mr Thornton in the corridor? I looked both ways down the corridor but it was empty, all the pupils were in their lessons, nobody to start a fight with. I suddenly noticed the fire extinguisher strapped to the wall with a Velcro strap, and in the heat of the moment it was the only thing I could think of.

I pulled the two black handles together and foam suddenly erupted from the nozzle like a jet and I screamed at the top of my voice, 'HELLLLLLPPPP!'

Mr Thornton rushed out the door, thankfully without the sword in his hand, and struggled to grab the hose pipe like a snake waving in the air of its own volition, but he couldn't stop it. There was no off-switch.

Pupils laughed and clapped standing in the door frame and looking from the windows as the foam filled the floor like the surf on a beach.

Other teachers stepped out from the door of their classrooms to see what all the commotion was about.

Mr Brompton and Miss Hardy rushed to help Mr Thornton and both slipped in the foam and landed on their backsides. I couldn't help laughing at the look on their faces. It was sheer pandemonium, with pupils from their classes running to skid in the foam, like the main corridor had suddenly become a seaside fairground attraction in the middle of Period 3.

Finally, the fire extinguisher was spent and Mr Thornton stood there covered up to his hands and knees in foam and panting for breath. He suddenly seemed to remember something, and rushed back into the room, and I followed him and watched him pick up the sword, run to his office and lock it back in the glass cabinet. I looked at Mason. He was the only pupil sitting quietly at his desk seemingly unaware of what all the fuss was about, smiling serenely. I knew he had it.

I suddenly heard the booming voice of Mr Winchester, the Deputy Head, 'back to your classes, NOW!' I think they could probably hear him on the East Wing and we were on the West Wing.

Pupils rushed back to their seats.

Mr Winchester appeared at the door and said, 'Mr Thornton, may I have a quiet word?' They stepped outside the door and closed it. We could see them talking animatedly and I was just counting the seconds before they called my name.

Mr Thornton walked back to the front of the class sheepishly.

'Alex, would you care to come outside,' Mr Winchester said, 'wait outside my office.'

I sat outside the Deputy Head's office where every teacher and pupil that passed could see that I was in trouble. It was the office right beside Miss Proctor's, and I dreaded her seeing me when her door opened. She closed the door behind her, and, of course, saw me.

I closed my eyes and prayed that she wouldn't come over. Of course, she came over.

'Good morning, Alex. What are you doing here?'

'I let off the fire extinguisher by accident. The whole corridor's flooded. I'm going to be expelled, I know it.'

'You're mind-reading again, Alex. It's a dangerous habit. Do I have your permission to talk to Mr Winchester? I won't give any details, just that you're dealing with a few domestic issues at the moment.'

'If you think it will help?'

'Don't worry, here he comes. Paul, could I just have a brief word?'

'I'm sorry, Hilary, I'm trying to deal with a fire extinguisher that's just gone off on the West Wing, and I have to speak to this boy. Can we talk over lunch?'

'It's about this,' she indicated me with her eyes, 'can we speak in private?'

They both went in and when she came out a few minutes later, she winked at me as I was called in.

There was a big open fireplace with flames rising from the coal, which was a bit ironic considering I'd just let off a fire extinguisher, a brass coal bucket filled to the brim, and three ornamental hanging brass tongs with different ends, like a poker, giant pair of scissors and a brush. Mr Winchester sat behind a wide mahogany desk with the windows behind him and two armchairs in front.

When he asked me what had happened, I admitted straight away that I had done it and apologised, but said it was an accident. I was only curious what the handle felt like when I came back from the toilet, and when it went off, I called for help straight away. I couldn't tell him I was helping to find a clue to save a missing boy's life.

'Do you realise it is a criminal offence to tamper with a fire extinguisher? Fire Extinguishers are our first line of defence in an emergency, especially in an old school like this. We normally hold an investigation in matters like this, call your parents in and ask them to pay for the damage, but I have just spoken to Miss Proctor, and I feel it is not appropriate in this instance. You would normally be suspended without any mitigating circumstances; do you understand that?

'Yes, sir.'

'I've agreed to give you a two-hour detention after school for three days. You can do your homework in the detention room. You should consider yourself a very lucky boy and make sure it never happens again. You may leave.'

'Yes sir, thank you.'

His bark was worse than his bite but it was far too close for comfort. I let out a deep breathe outside the door and realised I was shaking. Thank heavens for Hilary. Mason was right, she was a get-out-of-jail-free card and a half.

After all this, Mason better have the message.

I walked as quickly as I could without running back to our room.

CHAPTER TWENTY-SEVEN

The deal

Mason informed me in our room that fourth period was cancelled because of the fire extinguisher incident and we were all given study leave until lunch while it was cleaned up. I felt guilty thinking about the cleaning lady with her mop and bucket having to do more work because of us.

'I wasn't expecting a fire extinguisher,' he said.

'Did you really let it off on purpose, or was it an accident?' Sarah asked incredulously.

'Of course, I let it off on purpose. What else was I supposed to do? I feel bad about lying to Miss Proctor but I couldn't tell her why. She always says it's about making your own decisions.'

'What do you mean always? Have you been to see her?'

'I mean according to Mason ... No, I'm sick of lying. Yes, I went to see her. If I hadn't, I would've been suspended for this.'

'That's Karma,' Mason said, 'always follow the noble eightfold path. Or as Christians say, the truth shall set you free.'

'Why did you go and see her,' she asked sympathetically, 'was it about us?'

'What do you mean by us?' I said. Sarah blushed. 'You mean our search for Patrick Mackensie?'

'Yes, that's what I meant,' she said quickly, looking slightly flustered, 'exactly.'

'Of course, not. Nothing about that goes outside this room. This was personal stuff.'

'Can you leave him alone,' Mason said, 'he doesn't want to talk about it. And I've got a little surprise?' He held the small ball up in the air.

'Where did you find it?' Sarah said excitedly, 'give me it.' She snatched it out of his hand before waiting for a reply.

'It was sellotaped under the dagger display cabinet. If Mr Thornton moved the cabinet, it would have still been there. Very clever.'

She unwrapped it with her perfectly manicured fingernails, placing the Malteser on my desk. 'There's another squiggle. I think it's an L.'

'I knew it!' I said excitedly, grabbing my journal, and the Malteser, and showing her the list of six letter words I'd found beginning S.T.U., 'It's right here,' I munched, 'Stulte, Stulti, Stulto. It means fool!'

'Exactly,' Mason said drily, 'you are one. If the next letter is a T, you can have my share of the reward.'

'Is that a promise? Shake on it,' I said, 'Sarah is our witness.'

'No, I'm not shaking ...'

'See, you know I'm right. There's no other six letter Latin words beginning with S.T.U., I know, I checked.'

'OK,' he offered his hand, 'I'll shake on it.'

I gladly pumped his arm. 'You are going to be so sorry, my friend. You've just lost, wait a second,' I grabbed my calculator from the drawer and typed in 50,000 times 0.35, 'O.M.G. Seventeen thousand five hundred pounds. That's more money than I can imagine.'

'This is not about money,' he said, 'it's about a boy's life. What does the message say, Sarah?'

'*Nitimur in vetitum*. Did I say that right? But I don't know what it means.'

'Nitimur in we-tee-tum,' Mason said, '*We strive for the forbidden.*'

'What does *that* mean?' I said. It sounded ominous.

'Is it like Eve in the Garden of Eden wanting to eat the forbidden apple?' Sarah said. 'We all know what the apple is a symbol of.'

I frowned. 'I don't.'

'Yes, you do,' she pushed my shoulder, 'sex, of course.'

'Oh,' I felt embarrassed at the mention of the word. She couldn't be right, though, God wouldn't start the bible with something like that.

'It's from a poem by Ovid, I think,' Mason said, 'it means that when we can't have something, we eagerly look for what we can't have.'

'See, it doesn't have anything to do with ... that word,' I said.

'You're so naïve, Alex.'

'Will you two stop it. We need to work out which room it is.'

'What song is it?' Sarah asked.

I suddenly remembered we hadn't even played her the song yet. I checked my journal. 'Believer by Imagine Dragons. Play it on your laptop, Mason. And turn it up. You're going to love this song, Sarah.'

'Why, is it about SEX!' She shouted in my ear and laughed as I cringed. 'Boys are so immature.'

Which I thought was pretty immature, myself, and I was about to argue but the song started.

The drums started in an African pattern like war drums with a clap in between, like the tribe stomping their feet, a piano played an eerie octave single note, and a plaintive scared voice soared above like a boy facing the ritual of manhood. The voice said he wanted to tell everything he was thinking because he was tired of the way things were going on. He said he was broken since a child, and then a sound like a jet sucking the air back before he cried, 'PAIN' and whining electric guitars strung and he sung that was what made him a believer, over and over again. Until the last verse where he prayed to the one above and sung all the hate had made his spirit like a dove. He hoped his feelings would go away but they never would and rained like pain. The song faded out like him being sucked back in a cave.

'What is a believer?' Mason asked, as if he already knew which room it was.

'Someone who believes in God,' I said, 'he prayed to the one above in the song.'

'And where do we pray in the school?'

'In the school chapel,' Sarah said.

'Exactly,' Mason said, 'Come on, let's go. There isn't much time.'

We made haste for the chapel.

CHAPTER TWENTY-EIGHT

Suffering

I looked up at the statue of Jesus Christ on the cross with a crown of thorns behind the altar in the chapel with its stained-glass windows illustrating him carrying the cross on the way to be crucified. I heard the 'Believer' song in my head with its awful cry of pain like it was describing the crucifixion Jesus suffered for our sins, apparently.

'I don't understand why Christians wear a cross. It is the most painful event that could happen to a man.'

'He rose to heaven.' Sarah said.

'Then why not wear a symbol like a dove rising, rather than be reminded of his suffering all the time.'

'Life is suffering,' Mason said.

'I thought you were a Buddhist?'

'I am. That is Buddhism. How to escape the suffering of life and find nirvana. But it's very logical, not like Christianity. You don't

have to be a believer; you don't have to rely on Faith in some higher
power. The Buddha says question everything, even what he says.
You can only find out the answer by finding it yourself.'

'Do you believe in God, Sarah?' I asked.

'Of course, I do. It is logical,' she said, 'my mother said we may
have discovered the laws of physics but who created them in the
first place? It's *too* logical to be a coincidence. Do you?'

'My mother says I do, but I'm not sure, to be honest. I think I
do.'

'You have to open the door of your heart,' she said, 'and simply
ask Him, and He will answer.'

'Gobbledygook,' Mason said.

'No isn't,' Sarah said, 'He spoke to me, one day when I was really
sad and homesick and I prayed for my mother to collect me. He
said everything was going to be OK.'

I had never even thought of praying when I was homesick, and
felt guilty; maybe I wasn't a very good Christian.

'The Church was created to control us by making everybody
think they're a sinner,' Mason said, 'and they have to worship a
God to be saved. How can a baby be a sinner. Look at this place,
it's all about power. You believe what you want to believe, that's
the one thing nobody can control. But where is the message? We
haven't got time for a theological debate.'

'He mentioned a dove in the song,' I said.

'Over there.' Sarah pointed up at a large multi-coloured
stained-glass window in the right arched concave either side of the
altar, with rays of light pictured emanating from the dove. There

couldn't be a clearer sign in the whole chapel and we all sidled between the empty pews to reach it.

There was a sideboard with candles on it underneath. 'We should light a candle for Patrick Mackensie,' Sarah said, 'I'm going to come back later.'

'Stop talking and look for it,' Mason said, 'before someone comes in and asks us what we're doing.'

'We haven't got time,' I said, 'we're going to be late for Drama.'

'Quick as you can.' Mason said.

I knelt down on the rubber mat, made the sign of the cross to ask Him where it was. But first I had to say sorry for all the lies I'd told and ask for His forgiveness because I knew it was wrong. I asked Him to understand that I was trying to save a boy's life and to forgive me for thinking about the money so much. I told Him we didn't have any money but I knew that was no excuse. I asked him to look after Mason and Sarah if I left, and help my mother, if my father left. And finally, I asked where the Malteser was and waited for Him to answer, focusing on the picture of the dove in my mind's eye. There was no voice but I felt like I was looking down on us, and the candles were dots in the shape of an arrow pointing to the one at the front. I thanked Him, made the sign of the cross, and opened my eyes.

I looked at the candles from the side, and they *were* like two sides of an equilateral triangle staggered forward, it just didn't seem so from the front, or maybe it was my subconscious, but they were definitely pointing to the candle at the apex at the front.

But it was just a candle on a little flat bronze saucer, two inches radius, with a spike protruding from beneath, presumably going up into the candle. Mason was patting the walls with his palms, and Sarah was crawling around on the floor, as I stared at the candle.

How could he get a Malteser inside a candle, I thought, it was impossible. I must be wrong. *Look up*, I thought I heard someone say, *look up* ... I looked up into the high beams of the chapel roof, but then I thought, look up at the candle!

I crouched down and looked up at the candle and there was a little white ball pierced by the spike of the candle holder, hidden by the bronze saucer above.

'I've found it!' I cried, and gently pulled it down the spike and it dropped into the cup of my hand, as Mason rushed over. '

'Give me that,' Sarah reached me first, and snatched it out of my hand, 'I've got fingernails.' She had a bad habit of doing that, especially in a chapel.

She unwrapped the ball and handed me the Malteser. It had hole running through it and I looked at Mason through it. 'A *holy* Malteser, get it?'

'There's a squiggle.'

'Wait a second, don't say it,' I said, munching on the Malteser, 'remember what we shook on Mason. Sarah was our witness. If it's a T, you lose seventeen thousand five hundred pounds.'

Although I felt a bit guilty thinking about the money again, especially when I'd just apologised to Jesus for thinking about it too much. I wasn't really going to deprive him of his reward, I thought, that would be too cruel, but it was fun teasing him.

'I still say it's not going to be a T,' he said calmly, but he had to be bluffing, he must be nervous.

'Drum roll please, what letter is it, Sarah? Go on, tell him.'

'I'm sorry, Alex, it's definitely not a T. It looks more like a U.'

I was stunned, it couldn't be, 'Let me see that,' I took the torn paper off her. She was right. 'But I checked. There was only one word beginning S.T.U.L. that has six letters followed by a T; it doesn't make sense.'

'I said you were a fool; He who laughs last, laughs hardest.'

'The order must be wrong or something. Maybe we need to rearrange the letters.'

'Give me that,' Mason took the paper out of my hands, '*Verbum Domini lucerna pedibus nostris.* It means, the word of the Lord is a light for our feet,' Mason said.

'He's talking about his escape,' I said.

'Maybe,' Mason said, 'looking up at the statue of Christ on the crucifix. But the song was about pain. I think someone is causing him pain. Real physical pain, not just words. Remember the last message, Carthage must be destroyed.'

'You always scare me when you speak like that, Mason,' Sarah said.

'Sarah's right,' I said, 'I don't like this. It is too scary to think about.'

'We need to do something, not just talk about it,' Mason said, 'we need to find the last two clues and quick.'

'What is the last song?' Sarah said.

'Riptide.' Mason said.

'We can't play it in a church,' I said, 'that's disrespectful.'

Outside the chapel, the corridors were swarming with pupils like ants about their business as I scrolled down to Riptide on Mason's phone, handed Sarah the other wireless earpiece and pressed play.

A banjo started strumming and a lonesome voice, like a cowboy on the prairie, began to lament his fears about the dark, the dentist, and all his friends turning green before the bass drum kicked in and he howled like a wolf, 'ah-ooh, ooh, ah-ooh, ooh, ooh'. Straight into the chorus about a lady who was going to the riptide, the dark side, but he sang she was singing the words wrong. He quit his job and went to New York City while she stayed on the highest shelf. In the bridge, he sung she was destined for the movies, like Michelle Pfeiffer, before repeating the chorus about the riptide and the dark side.

'It's got to be a female teacher,' I said, 'who's an actress?'

'Miss Zaborowksi, the drama teacher,' Sarah said excitedly, 'the drama studio! But where?'

'The song said she was staying on the highest shelf. But there are no shelves in the drama studio, it's just an empty floor.'

'There is in the prop room,' Mason said, 'above the curtain rail for the costumes. But how do we get in there, *don't* let off another fire extinguisher, Alex.'

'I'll do it.' Sarah said. 'Leave it to me, Alex. Hurry up, we can't be late.'

We quick-stepped to the Drama studio, with Mason limping and struggling to keep up.

CHAPTER TWENTY-NINE

Macbeth

W e walked into the dark drama rehearsal studio surrounded by hanging black curtains in silence like entering a cave and sat cross-legged on the floor in a circle around Miss Zaborowksi sitting on a chair under a spotlight in a pointy witch's hat and shawl. She waited for the last pupil to enter, took the register and put her laptop under the chair.

'Macbeth Act One Scene 1. Stage Directions, thunder and lightning. A storm. Disruption. Distortion. Chaos. As three mischievous evil witches gather to while away their wicked plot stirring the cauldron,' she moved her fist in a circle, 'that controls servant Macbeth's destiny to be King. Chanting, 'Fair is foul, and foul is fair,' she crowed and cackled like a witch, what do you think this means, anyone? Alex?'

'It's an alliteration. Good is bad and bad is good, miss.'

'Excellent, Alex. From the outset, we have this theme of appearance versus reality. It reinforces the sense of confusion. In Scene three, we meet the witches again, as one returns from killing pigs ...'

I looked at Sarah and caught her staring straight back at me in the shadows.

'... They make a magic potion to put a curse on a sailor whose wife annoyed the witches, and change the weather at sea and he is ship wrecked on the way home. What does this show us anyone? Greg?'

'The witches are mean.'

'Yes, well done, the witches like to play around, they like to control people, they act like puppet masters of sorts,' she made her hands into claws and wiggled her fingers like they had strings attached, 'enter Macbeth from stage right,' she looks to the left as if he was coming in. 'So foul and fair a day I have not seen,' she said in a misgiving deep voice. Why does Shakespeare have him say that, anyone? Heather?'

'He's scared of the witches, miss.'

'That's right, well done, Heather. Shakespeare is making a connection with what the witches said in the beginning. If you want to get an A in drama, all you have to do is look for the connections in the script between the lines in different scenes and spot the underlying theme. Every single *word* is important and if you blink you might miss it.'

'Do you think there's an underlying theme beneath the messages?' I whispered to Sarah.

'The secret society in the woods, perhaps they're all connected.'

'Hail to thee, Duke of Gladis,' the first Witch prophesises, 'Hail to thee, Duke of Cawdor,' prophesises the second Witch, 'All hail Macbeth, that shalt be king hereafter!' The third Witch prophesises. Why do you think Shakespeare has the Witches prophesise, anyone? Sarah?'

'Is it a set-up, miss?' Sarah put her hand down.

'Very good, Sarah, Shakespeare's pre-empting what will happen. We know the Witches have special powers because the Sailor was ship-wrecked, but do you think they use them for good or evil, anyone? Howard?'

'Fair is foul, and foul is fair, miss. Evil.'

'Excellent, Howard, you're making the connection. Do you think Macbeth will be king? You're all nodding. But will it be good? You're all shaking your heads. We don't know yet, but it doesn't look good, does it?

'Now I want you all to separate into your groups and you're going to be the Witches and create a short three-minute scene prophesising about a pupil and what wicked fate you have planned for them. You have ten minutes before we all see your performances. Three-two-one, go.'

Everyone stood and shuffled into their groups finding a space on the floor to be together. I wasn't in Sarah's group, sadly, but across the room I saw her raise her hand.

'Can I get a Witch's hat like yours, miss.'

'Here, you can have mine.' She handed it to her.

'And one for Helen and Katy?'

'Use your imagination. You're acting, remember, you don't need props.'

'Please, miss. I can't be the only one in a Witches hat, it won't look real. Please? Just this once.'

'Oh, all right,' she handed her the key, 'just this once. And you're the last one to ask.' She raised her finger at us, but I was the only one paying attention among the busy plotting Witches, as I watched Sarah bravely carry the key to the Prop cupboard.

A few minutes later she reappeared carrying two Witch's hats. She didn't look at me or give me a sign or anything, just handed the key to miss, and gave the Witch's hats to her friends. Maybe she didn't find it, I thought, but if it wasn't there, there was nowhere else I could think of.'

After the lesson, I couldn't wait to ask her, 'Did you find it?'

She didn't say a word, just winked at me, and I let out a sigh of relief. It had been like waiting to go to the toilet.

'Don't open it here,' Mason suddenly said behind me, 'there's too many pupils around. Let's go to my room.'

'Our room,' I reminded him.

And off we hurried.

CHAPTER THIRTY

The vote

S arah twirled in the middle of the room and hopped up and down, waving the little ball in her hand.

'I did it, I did it, I did it! I found the last clue.'

'I'm not renegotiating if that's what you're thinking,' Mason said.

'Do you think there's an underlying theme connecting all the messages, Mason? Sarah said it might have something to do with the secret society in the woods?'

'I already said that. Of course it does, but I'm not sure what. We need to know who the other people in the woods are. Maybe the last message will be a clue. Open it, Sarah.'

'You haven't asked me how I did it? The shelf was full of hats and plastic swords and stuff but it wasn't there. I began to panic, throwing them all on the floor, but the shelf was bare. And then I remembered how he hid it under the candle holder in the chapel last time, and taped it under the dagger display cabinet before that. I felt under the shelf and it was sellotaped there. I'm a genius! I put all the stuff back. If I had looked at you when I came out, Alex, I would have jumped for joy, so I tried as hard as I could not to think about it, and just focused on the floor.'

'Can you please just open the message?' Alex asked tiredly, 'we haven't got all day. We have to find him now.'

Sarah sat down, unpeeled the torn paper and ate my last Malteser, 'There's another squiggle. It looks like an M?' I watched her munching it jealously.

'S.T.U.L.U.M. Stulum?' I said, grabbing my Latin dictionary. 'It isn't here. Let me check online. It came up immediately as the first item. 'It's here, it's here. It means *Stump*. Never trust a school dictionary. No wonder they used to tear them up! Erga, *towards*, stulum, the stump. But I'm stumped. Which room is that?'

'The trees in the courtyard?' Sarah said, 'But there are four? Which one?'

'He's not hiding under a tree in the middle of the courtyard,' I said.

'No. I know what it is,' Mason said, 'you should pay more attention in class, Alex. But what's the message first, to be sure. Give me it.'

Mason read, his eye opening wide and smiled like he was right, '*volo non fugia*. It means, *I fly but do not flee*. Of course!'

'Of course? What has that got to do with trees?' I said.

'Which room in this entire building is the only room you cannot flee from?'

'The detention room?' I said, 'but I know he's not hiding there, I've been there.'

'Let me make it easier for you,' Mason said, 'who won the headmaster's prize?'

'Patrick Mackensie, of course. We all know that.'

'And what is the headmaster's prize?'

'A trophy.' Sarah said.

'What else?'

'Wait a second,' I said, 'I think the prefect on my tour said something about that. Isn't it a guided tour of the dungeons below the school?'

'And what letters have we found?'

I checked my journal and read aloud, 'E.R.G.A.S.T.U.L.U.M.'

'Ergastulum. It means, *dungeon*.'

I felt a shiver run down my spine.

'O.M.G.' Sarah and I mouthed at each other.

'Let's go,' I said.

'We can't go in the middle of the school day in broad daylight,' Alex said.

'But he's been down there almost two weeks. He must be starving to death.'

'Alex and I will go after lights out,' Mason said.

'No way,' Sarah said, 'there's no way I'm missing out on this. I found the last message, that's the most important one.'

'It could be dangerous, Sarah,' I said, 'what if he's, you know ... dead?'

We all looked at each other and then at the floor. None of us knew how to handle that.

'Let's have a vote,' I said, 'we're all equal partners. But we must respect the decision of the majority. Agreed?' They both nodded. 'Raise your hand if you think Sarah should go?'

'Can I just say something first,' Sarah said, 'if you don't vote for me, Alex, I'll never speak to you again. Thank you, now raise your hand if you think I should go?' Sarah held her hand in the air and stared at me hard.

I looked at Mason with his hands firmly on his knees. The thought of Sarah never speaking to me again was too much, I could see she meant it. I slowly raised my hand.

Mason shook his head, 'Girls!'

'Sorry, Alex,' I said.

'Passed by majority decision. I'm going. What time do we leave and where shall we meet?'

'The door to the basement is at the end of the corridor on the lower ground floor where we have Textiles,' Mason said, 'in the North Wing, but it's locked. We need to get hold of the cleaner's keys again somehow.'

'She won't give them to us again,' I said, 'doesn't anybody else have a key?'

'I thought it was a storage room,' Sarah said, 'I've seen Miss Docherty come out of that door with fabrics. I've got Textiles last period, leave the key to me, if you're sure it's not a cupboard.'

'I'm sure,' Mason said, 'but don't go down without us. Just get the key. We'll rendez-vous outside the door after lights out, E.T.A.

midnight, when everyone's asleep, including the House Matron. Wear something black and I'll bring some food, just in case he needs it.'

Sarah opened the door to leave.

'Sarah,' I said, 'would you really never have spoken to me again?'

'A handsome boy like you? I'm not *that* crazy.'

Mason threw his arms up. 'I told you, girls!'

'Sarah,' I stopped her again and smiled, 'good luck.'

'I don't need luck,' she smiled, 'I'm a professional, now.'

She closed the door silently behind her.

CHAPTER THIRTY-ONE

What is the underlying theme?

The night I had worked so hard for, and sometimes thought may never happen, finally arrived. I set my alarm for eleven-thirty. I kept turning over unable to sleep thinking about all the messages and wondering if there was an underlying theme like in Macbeth in this morning's Drama class.

We knew what the messages meant separately, but what did they all mean together? And what did that say about the school or Patrick Mackensie?

I got out of bed quietly and fetched my journal and torch, so as not to wake Mason. I read them again under the duvet leaning the journal on my bent knees: *it's your fault; you're flogging a dead man; who benefits; I saw, I came, I conquered; if you want peace, prepare for war; Carthage must be destroyed; and you, Brutus; we*

strive for the forbidden; The word of the Lord is a light for our feet;
and, *I fly but do not flee.*

There was *You're flogging a dead man—pain; if you want peace,
prepare for war* and *Carthage must be destroyed—*war; *and you,
Brutus—*betrayal;*we strive for the forbidden—*danger; *The word of
the Lord is a light for our feet—*truth; *I fly but do not flee—*hope.

I wrote down pain, war, betrayal, danger, truth and hope. Where
did he get the pain from? His grades because he flunked his tests:
Pain= grades, I wrote. Who was he at war with? Who was the
enemy? The school, the *system*, Mason said: War=system, I wrote.
Who betrayed him? It wasn't his girlfriend, like Sarah said, he
didn't have one. It was all teachers, I thought. But he couldn't be
mad at all the teachers in the school, I thought, it had to be one of
the ones that taught us. If he was trying to tell us which one, how
would he tell us? I suddenly realised: he would leave a message in
their teaching room, of course.

I went back through my journal to where we had found the
messages and the teachers: The drama studio—Miss Zaborowksi;
The Chapel, which teacher? The Chaplain? But he wasn't a
teacher, it couldn't be him. The Maths room—Mr Thornton. He
was the leading man, the weaver of intricate lies in the song, it had
to be him, and I'd seen him in the ritual with my own eyes with
the nine other Witches. Wait a second, I thought, there were ten
songs, ten messages and ten witches! Patrick Mackensie was trying
to tell us who the ten witches were. Why hadn't we thought of that
before, it was staring us straight in the face.

I quickly flicked back through the pages: The Sports Pavilion—Mr Swanson; The art room—Miss Haversham; The Counselling room-Miss Proctor, *Hilary*, but she was a school counsellor? She couldn't be. I continued anyway: The Trophy cabinet—but which teacher? The headmaster's trophy, it couldn't be the headmaster? I felt scared, it couldn't be. I remembered him walking down the aisle in assembly with the policewoman. No, it couldn't be. I couldn't stop myself now: The Server room—which teacher? There wasn't a teacher, unless it was Mr Franks, the I.T. Technician? The Coat of Arms in reception—but which teacher, there was only Miss Lavender on reception? No way. And finally, the cornerstone—but which teacher? I remembered it was a boy, Elvis, who gave me the tour. It couldn't be him, but what was the Sales and Marketing Manager's name, who organised all the tours? Miss Pearl!

I closed my eyes and pictured them standing around the burning piglet, trying to imagine their faces under the masks, the bodies under the robes. I remembered there looked like five men, and five women.

I made a table with two columns, the women first: Miss Zaborowksi, Miss Haversham, Miss Proctor, Miss Lavender and Miss Pearl; Five.

And then the men: Mr Thornton, The Chaplain, Mr Swanson, The Headmaster, Mr Franks; Five.

Five women and five men <u>exactly</u>, I underlined it.

I was so happy at the thought of telling Alex and Sarah, and how impressed they'd be, I finally drifted off to sleep.

I was rudely awoken by someone shaking my shoulder, and tried to shrug it off, and get back to sleep.

'Leave me alone,' I mumbled, 'I'm sleeping.' I snuggled back under the warm duvet.

'Alex, wake up, we've got to go now. Sarah's waiting for us with the key.'

'What time is it?' I wearily opened my eyes, my head in a daze, wondering why Alex's face was painted brown.

'Quarter to midnight. The dungeon, we've got to go.'

I lifted the duvet off and sat on the edge of the bed like a zombie, 'Give me a second.'

I put on my black track trousers and hoody and fumbled with the laces of my trainers while Mason insisted on putting brown shoe polish on my face, too.

'Let's go quick,' he put on his backpack and grabbed his torch, 'before she thinks we're not coming.'

He opened the door and looked either way down the dark silent dorm corridor, held his thumb and forefinger in a ring like a scuba-diver,d put his finger to his lips and I followed him, sneaking into the darkness.

Chapter Thirty-Two

Midnight rendez-vous

We tiptoed past the sleeping dorm rooms careful not to make a sound on the creaking floorboards and wound our way down the spiral staircase lightly holding onto the rail as a guide.

We crouched our way along the side wall of the main school corridor, keeping below the window line of the empty classrooms either side until we reached the North Tower, and slowly descended to the lower ground floor.

We passed the Textiles room and when I shone my torch through the window, the faceless heads and legless bodies of mannequins stared back.

We reached the old door at the end of the corridor but there was no sign of Sarah.

I suddenly felt a tap on my shoulder.

'Boo!' She laughed stepping out of the shadows of the recessed alcove.

'That's not funny,' I hissed.

'Stop arguing. Did you get the key?' Mason whispered.

Sarah smiled holding a grey iron key, and a silver chub lock key in the air tied with string to a wooden placeholder, 'I volunteered to fetch the fabric. It was easy. She always asks pupils to get things for her because of her arthritic knees and the stairs. Follow me.'

She opened the door and I shone my torch on the descending stone steps and closed the door behind me. She flicked the light switch on and a single bare bulb lit the large blocks of the stone walls disappearing as they curved out of sight. I zipped up my black hoody, it was dank and colder as we crept down the steps.

At the bottom of the steps there was another corridor leading into the darkness, but no floorboards, only stone rocks, and a door.

'This is where she keeps the fabrics,' she said, opening it with the silver chub key and switched the light on. I looked up at the shelves with long cardboard tubes wrapped in fabric of every colour with different patterns on, fancy embroidered pillows, patchwork quilts, glass jars filled with pins, needles, clear plastic boxes of scissors, pencils and staple guns, boxes of large designer's sketch pads, a bin liner full of tea bags, collapsible tables and chairs stacked against another wall, and old sewing machines on the floor, 'he's not in here.' She closed the door.

Mason led the way continuing into the darkness with the beam of his torch casting our shadows on the wall, like strangers following us, until we reached a seven-foot-high black cast iron Victorian gate crossed with bars two inches thick and a foot apart.

There was a three-inch gap beneath the gate but it was far too narrow to squeeze under. There was an iron square plate with a keyhole the length of a biro and a heavy chain wrapped twice around the handles with a padlock.

'There's no way he could have got passed this,' I pulled the chain and the rattle echoed. 'The police must have checked how secure this is.'

Mason shone his torch through the bars into the empty cavernous space with doors leading off it.

'What's that over there?' I said, noticing rocks glinting against the wall. We trained our beams on a mountain of coal against the wall.

'What's that?' Sarah shone her torch on the wall opposite. There was a giant iron machine, twice the height of a teacher, with little doors above and below a big door the height of pupils and a grill on the front like mouths with metal teeth, with round gauges above like eyes, and large thick pipes running vertically right up into the ceiling like medusa's hair of snakes.

'It must be a furnace,' Mason said, 'to heat the school. Doesn't look like they use it any more. He must have found a way in.'

'He did,' Sarah said, 'the headmaster's prize. But they didn't leave him. He can't be here, let's go back. This place gives me the creeps.'

'No, this might be the only chance we have.' He pulled against the bars and they rattled against the chains. 'Ergastulum means dungeon. He *must* be here.'

'Forget it, Mason,' I said, 'Sarah's right. It's impossible. Unless he really was a ghost and just floated right through the bars.'

Mason lifted the padlock which was almost the size of his hand and raised the little sliding key cover before shaking his head and dropping it, 'it's improbable not impossible. Remember what Sherlock Holmes said, when you have eliminated the impossible, whatever remains, however improbable, must be the truth.'

'I grabbed the bars of the gate with both hands and shook it. 'This is not improbable, Mason. It's impossible. Let's get out of here before someone finds us down here.'

'Be still, Alex, and just listen.' He sat down in the lotus position, rested the back of his palms on his knees holding his thumbs and forefingers together, lifted his chin and closed his eyes.

'Oh, no,' I looked at Sarah, 'he wants to meditate.'

I slumped down to sit on the hard and cold stone floor in the gloom, we could be here for hours, and Sarah sat down too. If anyone came down now, I thought, we were sitting ducks.

I tried to think of somewhere else Patrick Mackensie could be, but there weren't any more clues. We had exhausted every room on the list. There was no pot of gold at the rainbow, just this. Staring at the bars I felt like I was in prison.

'He couldn't have survived long down here,' I said to Sarah, 'even if he did get past the gate. Do you think they locked him in?'

Mason suddenly opened his eyes, 'I've got it!'

We both crawled over to him on our hands and feet like spiders.

'How did he get in?' I said urgently.

'I had a lucid dream. I could see him falling down from the sky through the ceiling and the rocks falling around him as he landed and there was this big hole in the roof looking up to the sky and he was covered in dust.'

However ridiculous it sounded I shone my torch on the ceiling, 'there's no big hole in the ceiling, Mason. It's a stone roof, he couldn't have fallen through that.'

'Lucid dreams are not necessarily literal. It could be a trapdoor.'

'The ceiling must be twenty-foot high,' I said in exasperation, 'he would have broken his legs.'

'Maybe he made a rope ladder?'

I scanned the ceiling again for a trapdoor but there was nothing. My torch rested on the mountain of coal and I suddenly pictured the coal truck parked outside the night I returned from the woods and saw the wide yellow chute plugged into the side of the building.

I slowly raised the beam of my torch and half way between the top of the stack and the ceiling, there was a large dark man-sized cast iron funnel leading upwards at a slant.

'I've got it!' I cried, 'Look over there, the coal chute!'

'That's it,' Mason said, 'it's a hole looking up to the sky. I *knew* it. There must be a door outside.'

'I know where it is,' I said, 'I saw the truck delivering coal that night.'

'Let's go now,' Sarah said, 'while they're still asleep.'

We rushed after Sarah, past the Textiles storage door and back up the stone steps.

CHAPTER THIRTY-THREE

Slide to the moon

I showed Mason and Sarah to the place where I had seen the coal truck outside the North Tower, and sure enough there was an ornate black iron metal plate about four feet square with a handle.

'It's bound to be locked,' I tried the handle and it opened with a creek. 'What do we do now?'

We all looked at each other.

'Ladies first,' Ma on extended his arm gentlemanly.

'I'm not going in there, I'll ruin my hair.'

'Girls!' Mason shook his head ruefully.

'That does it,' Sarah said defiantly, gripped the top of the opening with one hand, climbed in feet first and screamed as the gravity pulled her down.

'Sarah,' I yelled down after we heard a thump, 'are you OK?'

'Remind me next time to bring a cushion but I'm fine, just a few scratches. Come down. It's fun.'

I shone my torch down the chute but it was curved and I couldn't see her. I heard the sound of falling rocks, and pulled my hoody up. I climbed in with both hands on the top of the opening, 'Wish me luck!'

I let go and went sliding down feet first and landed sorely on my bottom on lumps of coal, and quickly clambered down the pile, rocks of coal falling to the floor.

Mason was next and we all brushed the soot off our hair, legs and arms.

It was like landing on the moon with all the dusty rocks and cold stone floor.

I shone my torch up the high iron monster furnace. Standing up close to it, it seemed even bigger. I followed the pipes up into the ceiling and around the side. It was built into a corner, and there was a tap on the wall about waist height. I turned it and water suddenly splashed out onto my shoes.

'It's still working,' I said, 'at least he didn't die of thirst.'

'It must be a steam furnace,' Mason said looking up at the monster, 'and heated the whole building.'

'Only one slight problem,' I said, looking at the other side of the locked gate, 'how are we going to get back?'

'Let's worry about that if we find him.' Mason said.

'Don't worry, Alex,' Sarah said, 'I can always scream.'

I looked around at the heavy stone walls. 'Do you think anybody would hear you?'

'Follow me,' Sarah said and walked bravely ahead shining her torch down the tunnel and I was right behind her followed by Mason limping in the rear.

Sarah stopped at the first door and opened it nervously. She tried the light switch and it worked. The small windowless room was empty save for a rusty steel bunk bed full of cobwebs without a mattress, an empty open fire place and a sink.

I turned the tap on the sink and heard the pipes chugging, like it was clearing its voice, and then dirty brown water ran out.

'The furnace workers must have lived down here in Victorian times,' Mason said.

'That must have been awful,' Sarah said, 'it's like a prison cell.'

'I don't know. It's got a fire,' I said, 'at least they weren't cold.'

'He's not here,' Mason said, 'come on.'

Sarah and I followed Mason taking the lead to the last door.

He opened it carefully and turned the light on. We looked over his shoulder at the toilet. It had a square wooden seat with a hole in it and the cistern was high above with a pipe leading down to the bowl.

I walked in and looked into the bowl out of curiosity. It was longer and deeper than a modern toilet with water in the bottom.

'He's not in there,' Mason said.

I pulled the cord hanging down from the cistern and the toilet flushed, 'it still works!'

'It's just a toilet, Alex, it must be plumbed into the sewer. Maybe there's a way out through the sewer.'

'I'm not going in a sewer,' Sarah crinkled her nose up.

'You wouldn't fit down the toilet,' I stepped out, turned the light off and closed the door. 'That's it then, he's not here,' I said, 'get ready to scream, Sarah.'

'Wait a second,' Mason said, his torch catching something move in the shadows at the end of the tunnel.

A large brown rat the size of a kitten suddenly ran towards us and Sarah screamed. I pulled her aside just in time and it ran straight past us.

'Relax, I'm a Buddhist,' Mason said, 'I'm obliged by my vows to hurt no living being, and no living being will hurt me. Come on, it came from over there.'

'It was massive,' I said, 'you don't think it's just eaten something … Or someone?'

Mason walked slowly forward scanning the ground with each step until he suddenly seemed to disappear in the blackness.

I continued walking and realised he had just turned the corner and there was another corridor with a door at the end with light streaming from underneath.

'I think there's someone there,' Mason whispered.

Sarah grabbed my arm, 'Let's go back and call the police. We'll still get the reward if they find him. There might be someone keeping him there and if we disturb them, they might keep us.'

'If we need to scream to get out of here,' I said, 'you don't think they're going to hear us? And we're on *their* side of the locked gate. We're damned if we do, we're damned if we don't. Give me your hand,' I felt her sweet palm in mine, 'we'll be OK, Sarah, I promise.

I'll protect you. I don't care how big they are, I may go down, but I always get back up.'

'You're my hero, Alex.' Sarah said, squeezed my hand, and mouthed the words under the torch light, 'I love you.'

'Don't worry, everybody,' Mason said, 'I'm a trained Buddhist.'

'You do martial arts?' I said admiringly.

'No, I meditate. No living being will hurt me.'

I thought it wasn't the right time to mention his accident.

'Let's do this,' I said with resolve.

We all stepped slowly forward, careful not to make the slightest sound, until we finally reached the door and Mason knocked on it.

'Come in,' a voice said, 'I was expecting you.'

Mason slowly opened the door.

CHAPTER THIRTY-FOUR

Aladdin's cave

It was like opening a door on Aladdin's cave:

Purple silk sheets like a parachute billowed from the ceiling, the walls were draped with a fabric of elaborate gold curlicues on a red background pinned with beautiful sketches of lambs and baby animals.

There was an assortment of overlapping square patches of carpet on the floor in front of the burning open fire with flames rising from the coal.

The bunk bed was adorned with a velvet green curtain like a theatre stage opening with a bow at the biggest side and tied up in the corners and wrapped around the sides. Cushions were placed all around the lower bunk above a patchwork quilt, like a couch.

Net curtains hung on the back wall over tin-foil windows, with dainty curtains either side, under which three small collapsible tables were placed making a long table between the bunk and basin, full of coloured pencils and sketch pads of work-in-progress at which sat Patrick Mackensie.

His long hair hung over his shoulders and he was wrapped in an improvised blue silk Kimono and batik elephant pants with clean bare feet.

'Wow,' Sarah side, her eyes opening wide as she stared around the room.

'Do you like it?' Patrick asked.

'I love it,' she said, 'this is better than my room. How did you ...'

'I came down to fetch supplies for Miss Docherty the day I left, wrapped everything in in black sheets so they wouldn't be seen, and passed them under the Victorian gate. Please take a seat and make yourselves comfortable.'

We sat on the lower bunk-bed, it was very soft, he must have made a mattress from cushions. I looked at the basin in the corner opposite with a toothbrush, toothpaste, soap and a clean white towel hanging from the bracket. He had everything he needed. I had expected to find a starving emaciated or dead body crawled up on the stone floor. I could never have imagined this.

'Where are my manners,' he said, standing, 'I'm not used to having visitors. Would you like a cup of tea?' We all nodded and he lifted the iron kettle by the fireplace onto a metal grill above the fire with an improvised tea-towel, 'you must be exhausted discovering all the witches.'

Mason looked at me with a frown and said, 'What witches?'

'There wasn't time to tell you,' I said, 'the teachers in the rooms we found are the witches I saw in the woods.'

'I'm sorry,' Patrick said, 'I thought it was obvious. You must have lots of questions.'

'Yes,' Sarah said, 'how do you shower? I don't mean to be rude; you look very clean.' I watched her eyes look him up and down, playing with her hair flirtatiously.

'There's no shower. I put boiling water in that bowl over there, and have a bed bath. It's not ideal, but it stops B.O. from attracting the rats when I go to the toilet. Don't worry, they don't come in here.'

'We saw one,' I said, 'it was massive.'

'I recognise Sarah and Mason, but if you don't mind me asking, who are you?'

'I'm sorry. My name's Alex.'

He shook my hand, 'pleased to meet you, Alex. So, you are the brains of this outfit.'

I felt my face flushing, 'not really, we're a team. Mason is in charge; Sarah just thinks she is.'

'Don't say that about me, I was the first one down the chute,' Sarah said, 'I am *not* bossy.'

'See what I mean?' I said, and she gave me a foul look. So much for love.

'How do you eat?' Mason asked.

'I boil rice in the kettle. I stole ten bags of rice, a carton of chicken gravy and a spoon, bowl and mug from the kitchen. It was all I could fit in my school bag. And these,' he held up a packet of Maltesers from the bag, 'when I left the message in Hilary's office, I stole a dozen packets. Would you like one?'

Mason declined, 'No thanks, I'm sick of them.'

'Me too,' he said, 'Alex?'

'Yes, please,' I said, gratefully receiving the packet. I could never be sick of Maltesers and popped one in my mouth. Fresh and delicious.

The kettle whistled and he put a tea bag into a mug on the carpet in front of the fire and carefully poured. 'I'm afraid I haven't got any milk or sugar. But you get used to it. I've only got the one mug, who's first? Are you sure? OK, I'll have it. I've got so many questions myself. I thought you'd never come, but now we can start. There isn't much time, you need to get back before they notice you're missing, and I can't do it alone.'

'What do you mean, start?' I said, 'We've found you; it's finished.'

'You don't think I came down here for nothing. I need your help. The future of the farm and all the baby animals are at stake.'

I seemed to remember Elvis saying that the farm was closing because a fox was stealing the lambs and baby pigs and then I remembered the piglet being burnt alive in the woods, and I was desperate to find out more, as he casually sipped his tea and started to explain his story.

CHAPTER THIRTY-FIVE

Find the fox

I t turns out we were totally wrong about Patrick Mackensie's motivation for escape. He didn't leave because he was flunking in school, he left to highlight the plight of the missing animals from the farm.

'It's animal cruelty,' Patrick said, 'they can't talk for themselves. Someone had to do something.'

'Why didn't you start a petition, or organise a protest outside the farm?' Sarah said.

'And accuse the teachers of murdering them?'

'Why didn't you go to the police?' I said.

'I didn't have any evidence. Just my word against theirs.'

'How did you know the teachers were doing it?' Alex said, 'and who they were?'

'It's a long story. I used to visit the farm when I was in juniors and feed the lambs milk from a bottle. Last year, I realised every month another baby would go missing. They said it was a fox. I cried in my room feeling helpless until one night I resolved to catch the fox myself. I filled my parka pocket with little pebbles from the school drive as ammunition and took the slingshot I use for fishing. That thing can get a ball of ground bait from one side of the lake to the other. At close range, it is deadly and I'm a perfect shot.'

'I'm a Buddhist,' Mason said, 'I don't believe in any form of violence.'

'I'm a vegetarian,' Patrick said, 'and I love animals, but this was like cruelty to children and they are going to close the farm and all the animals will be slaughtered.'

'I want to be a vegetarian,' Sarah said, 'that's so cool.'

'I sneaked out an hour after lights out in my fishing balaclava. Foxes can see the light reflected on your face. I used my phone as a compass to make my way through the woods so I wouldn't be seen on the path. I crouched in the bushes less than ten metres away from the lambs' pen and waited. Nothing. No fox. After a few hours I went back and determined to try again the following night. I kept returning night after night, until I was so used to the way through the woods, I didn't need my phone compass, trying out different hiding spots. And then one night ...

'You saw the fox?' Sarah said.

'No. I saw teachers arriving in their cars and parking in the farm car park. First, Mr Swanson and Miss Pearl. Then Mr Thornton and Miss Zaborowski, then the Chaplain and Miss Haversham. But they weren't going inside, just standing together carrying coats or something over their forearms, waiting for somebody. And then Mr Winchester pulled up in his black Mercedes 8 series, I recognised it immediately, and got out with Miss Proctor, Miss Lavendar and Mr Franks, who took a big box out of the boot and carried it for Mr Winchester.'

'I thought it was the headmaster,' I said, 'because of the headmaster's trophy. Mr Winchester gave me a detention.'

'Sorry, I thought you'd have known that Mr Winchester organises the headmaster's prize, the headmaster just gives it out. Anyway, I thought why are they meeting outside the farm in the middle of the night? Perhaps they were having a meeting to discuss the closing of the farm, but only Mr Thornton and Mr Swanson walked away. I saw them open the gate to the lambs' pen. Mr Franks pulled out a gun, walked up to a little defenceless baby lamb and shot it in the head at point blank range. The shot rang out like an echo over the fields and I thought the whole world must have heard it. The lamb collapsed to its feet. Mr Swanson was the fox. The little lamb didn't stand a chance.

'They slipped on the robes they were carrying and headdresses over their heads and eyes, but it was too late, I had already seen their faces. Mr Swanson lifted the lamb onto Mr Thornton's shoulders, and he held it by the legs around his chest. When they got back to the group in the car park, they were all dressed and waiting in the same robes and proceeded to march in pairs into the woods, half with daggers on ropes around their waists. I don't know what happened after that because as soon as they were gone, I ran the other way back through the woods the way I'd come. I didn't care what they were doing, all I could think about was them murdering that little baby lamb. They had to be stopped, but I didn't know where to turn. I usually talk to Miss Proctor, she likes to be called Hilary ...'

'We know.' Mason and I said simultaneously.

'But she was one of them. I couldn't believe it; the school counsellor. It was like a nightmare. I thought what would people think if instead of baby lambs going missing, a pupil went missing, without running away, a total mystery. The more the mystery, the more they would have to investigate. If only I could find a way of sharing their identities, everyone would point the finger at them. That's when I came up with the idea of their teaching rooms.'

'Why didn't you just leave a list of their names?' Mason said.

'And then what? They would just be my teachers' names. I needed to send a message about the war of cruelty to animals, and their betrayal, but I knew nobody would believe me if I simply put it in a letter and, worst of all, they would blame me for pointing the finger. And I didn't want to give them the opportunity to make excuses straight away and say it was all my imagination. I needed to find a way to drip-feed the messages over time, and patiently wait while all the teachers were discovered one-by-one, and put all the pieces together; they were in this *together*. Although Mr Swanson pulled the trigger, they are all guilty in my book.'

'I have a question,' I said, 'and I think this is the most important one, to be honest, Patrick. Why the Maltesers?'

'I wanted to show the messages were from the same person, and not just random scraps of paper that could be from anywhere.

Like Zorro slashing a Z with his sword, Maltesers were my secret identity.'

'Why in Latin?' Sarah asked, 'I didn't understand them.'

'I didn't want you to, I wanted whoever found them to be smart enough, or ask someone who was smart enough, to figure them out, and not just throw them away,' I saw Sarah look down at her feet, 'that must be you, Alex.'

'No, it was Mason,' I said

Mason shrugged modestly, 'I know a bit of Latin.'

'Why didn't you think they were about the teachers? That was the whole point.'

Mason also looked down sadly, 'I suppose I didn't meditate well enough; I'm only a novice.'

'Don't criticise Mason,' I said, standing and clenching my fists, 'if it wasn't for him, we wouldn't be here. And who are you to call Sarah not smart enough? She didn't flunk every test except for Art and Latin.'

'I won the headmaster's prize,' Patrick said defensively.

'Who cares about the headmaster's prize. What good is service to the community if you're not kind to people and have respect? They're the heroes for figuring out how your mind works, not you with your silly puzzles.'

Patrick held up the palms of his hands, 'I'm sorry, I'm sorry.'

'Don't apologise to me, apologise to them,' I pointed at them.

'Hey, I'm sorry if I caused any offense, Sarah and Mason. Is that OK, Alex?'

I sat down, 'We didn't even know if you were alive and we'd find a dead body down here.'

'What about your parents, Patrick?' Sarah said, 'they must be so worried. We've got to tell them you're OK.'

'NO! Then it's all been for nothing. Please help me. I'm only trying to save the baby animals. If we don't do anything,' he pointed at his drawings on the wall, 'they're all going to die.'

'I think you've very brave,' Sarah said, 'I can't speak for the others, but I want to help.'

'What's the plan?' Mason said.

'Are you in, Alex?'

I hesitated and smiled, 'who doesn't love baby animals.'

Chapter Thirty-Six

No way out

'We need evidence to go to the Police,' Patrick said.

'Why didn't you take a video with your phone?' Sarah said.

'I keep asking myself the same question. I don't know, it all seemed to happen too quickly. I suppose I was in shock.'

'I saw them burning a piglet alive,' I said, wincing at the memory, 'and chanting in something like Latin in some kind of ritual in a circle.'

'That must be why they're murdering the animals; a sacrifice to the Gods. Did you take a video?'

'No. Mr Thornton spotted me and came after me with a long dagger on his belt.'

'We *need* evidence,' Patrick repeated urgently.

'That's two witnesses,' Sarah said, 'surely the police can't ignore you.'

'They're not going to believe a bunch of kids versus ten teachers, including the Deputy Head and school counsellor, without any evidence,' Mason said. 'Patrick's right, we need evidence. Do you remember where you saw them?'

'There was a clearing in the middle of the woods. I don't know exactly, I remember which way I ran to the woods, but I didn't use a compass or anything. I think I could trace the way back.'

'How do we know if they'll go back?' Sarah asked.

'A baby animal goes missing every month,' Patrick said, 'I saw them on a Sunday night, a month ago. How about you?'

I thought for a moment. 'Yes, it was a Sunday night, last Sunday.'

'That means they're going to be back on a Sunday,' Mason said, 'in four weeks.'

'There's not enough food for us to stay down here that long,' I said, 'we've got to find a way out of here.'

Patrick shook his head, 'there isn't one. The only way out is the gate and if they open that they'll find me and it's all over. We'll have to tell them everything, and it will be our word against theirs.'

'What about the coal chute?' I said.

'I know,' Patrick said, 'that's how I got in, I noticed it on the tour when I won the headmaster's prize. But it's slippery with soot and practically vertical. I once tried to go and steal more food, there's nothing to grip onto.'

'I forgot,' Mason said, opening his bag, 'I brought you some sandwiches. Is cheese and ham, OK? I didn't know you were a vegetarian.'

Patrick's eyes lit up at the sight of them and he ripped open the cling film and stuffed them into his mouth like a dog, 'I never thought a ham and a cheese sandwich could taste so good.'

'I can drop some more food down the chute now we know where you are,' Mason said, 'if we can get out?'

'We could make a ladder,' I said, 'using the wood from the chairs and tables.'

'I haven't got any nails,' Patrick said chewing a mouthful.

'We could use the screws from the tables and chairs,' I said.

'I haven't got a screwdriver.'

'Have you got a knife?'

'No, but I've got a spoon,' he held it up. I grabbed it and tried to twist the screw with the curve of the rounded end but it had no purchase.

'What about scissors?' Sarah said, handing me them from the table, but the point of the scissors had no purchase either. I put my hands on my hips and looked around the room at the fabrics hanging from the wall and ceiling.

'I've got it!' I said excitedly. 'A grappling hook.'

'There isn't any rope.' Patrick said.

'We could pull down these sheets, and tear them into strips,' I said.

'There isn't any hook?' Patrick said.

I looked around the room.

'The chair leg! We break it off, tie it to the sheets, and throw it up and catch it either side of the door. You didn't close it did you, Mason?'

'No, but the door is on one side, it's impossible.'

'Not if we get the angle right,' I said, 'there's a wall below and to the right.'

'The chute is diagonal and bends,' he said, 'we'd never be able to throw a chair leg around a bend, never mind up that high.'

I sat down flummoxed for a solution, 'We've got to get out of here somehow. Have you got a better idea?'

'Yes,' he said, sitting down on the floor in the lotus position, placed the back of his open palms on his knees, lifted his chin level and closed his eyes.'

'What's he doing?' Patrick asked.

I rolled my eyes, 'Meditating!'

'Shhh,' Sarah said, pointing her finger at him.

We all sat there waiting and I looked around the room thinking as hard as I could, how we could use the resources we had. Every problem had to have a solution, I reminded myself, just like solving for X in Algebra. X was the way out, what were the known values and the variables?

'What if we never get out of here?' Sarah whispered in my ear, 'and we run out of food.'

'Don't think like that,' I whispered back, 'in a crisis you've got to stay positive.' Although I couldn't help thinking, what if she was right, and there was no way out, after she'd said it; fear was contagious.

Mason finally opened his eyes with a serene smile, 'I've got it.'

'Thank goodness for that,' I sighed louder than I had expected. 'What is it?'

'I'm looking at it.' He smiled at each of us in turn, 'I had a lucid dream. We were building a ladder to the sky ... standing on each other's shoulders.'

'That's brilliant,' I said, 'why didn't I think of that.'

'You weren't thinking outside the box. That's what meditation does. You just breathe, let your mind be totally clear, and let the solution come to you, without forcing it in any way.'

'It just might work,' Patrick said, 'I couldn't do it alone, but maybe together ...'

We all rushed out the door.

CHAPTER THIRTY-SEVEN

The great escape

We stood in front of the mountain of coal and shone our torches up at the opening of the coal chute.

'Patrick's biggest,' Sarah said, 'and he's staying, so he has to go at the bottom. You, Alex, are next, then me, and then Mason, he's the lightest, at the top.'

'At the top? I don't think this is going to work,' Mason said, 'it's too high up. I could break my neck. We call could. Maybe I should meditate again,'

'If Mason gets out, how will he be able to pull us up?' I said. 'He's not strong enough.'

'That's easy,' Sarah said. 'We'll use your idea but in reverse. He'll tie the anchor chair leg around the opening when he's out, lower it down and we'll climb out. Break off a chair leg and tie sheets together with a loop around it, and make knots in it, to climb up. Come on.'

We ran back to Patrick's room, while Alex stayed looking worryingly up at the chute.

Patrick and Sarah pulled the sheets off the ceiling and walls to make the rope, while I grabbed the folding chair.

I turned it upside down with the back and the sliding seat making a triangle with the floor.

I gripped the cross bracket of the highest pair of legs in the air and jumped on the cross bracket of the lowest legs.

There was a loud crack as the metal crossbar under the seat fractured the legs and the crossbar I was leaning on suddenly fell down like a guillotine, just missing my feet.

The seat was only connected to the frame by two small bolts now, and I laid it out flat like an ironing board against the lower bunk. I jumped on it, and there was a loud crack as the frame snapped.

The chair was in two pieces: one seat sliding between two sides, and one H frame, with the high back crossbar. I rested the H frame against side the bunk bed and sat bumping on it until the joint snapped and I fell to the floor. I grabbed the longest piece of wood, which was wide and strong enough to cross the chute opening and support us.

Mason came in and sat on the lower bunk looking worried and doing nothing.

When Patrick and Sarah had finished, I attached the improvised purple and pink silk rope to the wooden bar, and wrapped it all around and stuffed it into Mason's backpack.

We ran back to the coal mountain and scrambled to the top. The entrance was about three feet up the wall above the stack.

Patrick leaned his shoulders backwards into it, as I stood on his knees and clambered up into the pitch-black darkness until I was leaning back in the chute with my feet on his shoulders.

'Come on, Sarah,' I called down.

'Fast,' Patrick said, as she climbed up on him, 'my back is killing me.'

I suddenly felt Sarah's hands on my legs and then pulling on my jacket, and then the weight of her body as she pulled herself over me and finally her feet pressing into my shoulders.

'I can almost touch the opening,' Sarah said, 'come on, Mason.'

My body started to shake with the weight of Sarah on my shoulders, even though we were half-lying down at forty-five degrees, and I could feel Patrick's shoulders wobbling, as Mason clawed his way up him and grabbed my ankles.

'Hurry up, my legs are going,' Patrick said.

I tried to reach down to help in but I couldn't with Sarah digging into my shoulders. Mason crawled up me.

Sarah squealed, 'not there.'

'Sorry, Sarah,' Mason said, and a few moments later, 'I'm out!'

And just at that second, the floor seemed to disappear from under me and I fell down flying at twice the speed I had before, with the weight of Sarah's whole body pushing me down on top of mine, and crashed on Patrick with Sarah landing on top of me.

We all lay there groaning in a breathless mess and I looked up and slowly saw the purple and pink knotted rope descending.

'Come on,' Sarah jumped to her feet, 'we can do this.' She pulled herself up the rope between her knees, resting her feet on each knot before she pulled herself up to the next one and out of sight. Her voice echoed down the chute, 'I'm out.'

I took a deep breath, and pulled on the rope to check it was secure, 'Wish me luck.'

'Good luck,' said Patrick, 'and thank you for everything.'

'I promise I'll be right back to get you, OK? As soon as we've got the evidence.'

'You're a good man, Alex.'

'So are you, Patrick. So are you.'

I tested the rope again and then pulled myself up and climbed as Sarah had done.

My arms strained to heave myself to the next knot which was a lot more difficult than it looked watching from below. The knot seemed tiny beneath my feet and I feared the rope would give way every time I pulled myself to the next one.

When I finally saw Mason and Sarah's faces reflecting in the moonlight, I heard Patrick shout up, 'Don't forget the animals,' before I pulled myself out through the opening crawling on my hands in the mud until my legs were free and lay down on my back looking up at the stars trying to get my breath back. I was free.

Mason and Sarah were covered head-to-toe in soot. 'You look like chimney sweeps.'

'So do you,' Sarah said. We all laughed with relief.

'My hair is ruined,' Sarah said, 'I need to have a shower.'

'You always look good to me,' I said.

'Do you want to join me?' She teased.

'Will you two knock it off.' Mason said, standing up and dusting himself down. 'You know if they find him before we get the evidence,' he walked off, 'there won't be any reward.'

Mason was right, all we had to do now was get the evidence, and face my worst nightmare for the final time.

I ran after him beside Sarah. The reward was so close I could almost touch it.

CHAPTER THIRTY-EIGHT

The hunt for evidence

After weeks of dropping sandwiches and messages down the chute to Patrick every night, it was finally the Sunday we'd been waiting for. Mason and I were dressed in our black tracksuits and shoe polish after lights out, sitting on our beds, nervously waiting for Sarah and the end of the hour to go and get the evidence so Patrick could be free.

'Do you think we should bring a weapon for self-defence?' I said.

'I'm a Buddhist, Alex. Buddhists don't carry weapons.'

'I'm not. What if they come after us with their daggers?'

There was a gentle tap on the door and it opened slightly, 'Are you decent?'

Sarah stepped in wearing a black hat, black coat, black dress, black tights and pink wellington boots, somewhat defeating the object.

'Mason doesn't think we should bring any weapons.'

'Are you kidding?' Sarah said. 'We're not the SAS! We're reporters. Journalists don't carry weapons.' She waved her iphone in the air, 'our weapon is our camera. Have you checked yours is set to video.'

'I almost forgot,' I said thumbing through the phone settings.

'And set it to night-time mode, obviously, and turn down the light on the screen display, so it doesn't give us away when you turn it on.'

'Of course,' Mason took out his phone to change his settings.

'Boys!' She tutted, 'You forget the most important thing. We'll go to the farm first, we need to catch them in the act of killing.

'Alex, you lead the way, use Google maps, not your torch.

'Mason, you follow him, we can't have you falling behind with your limp, and I'll take the rear.

'If we get separated for any reason, head back here, don't go on alone or look for us.

'Remember what Patrick said, there are bushes near the animals' pen and farm car park, we'll hide in them.

'After that, we'll follow them to the clearing in the woods. Once we've got what we need, I'll give the signal to leave.

'If any of us are spotted, this is important, we all leave in different directions. Mason, head for the farm, it's bound to be closest, Alex head for the school, it's bound to be furthest, and I'll head for the main road and try and stop traffic if I have to.

'Finally, head back to this room, and if anyone is not here an hour later, call the Police. 999. It's an emergency. Are we all clear?'

Mason and I nodded.

'Let's go.' Sarah said.

I opened the door and checked the dorm corridor both ways before tiptoeing down it, followed by Mason and Sarah. We descended the staircase and sneaked down the empty main corridor of the North Wing and outside into the field in the night sky, past the stables and into the woods towards the farm.

It started to rain and the ground became wet and muddy under foot as we stumbled through the woods.

I could see our location on google maps but it was indicating the path which we couldn't use and I had to guess the direction to the farm.

We finally sat on our haunches in the bushes opposite the pen and in clear view of the car park, phones at the ready, and Sarah held her finger to her lips for us not to speak.

We waited in silence for what seemed like an eternity, and I thought we had the wrong Sunday and it was going to be a no-show, when I heard the sound of tyres on gravel, and the first car pulled around the side of the farmhouse and parked less than a hundred metres away, directly in front of us.

I trained my binoculars on the vehicle and saw Mr Thornton, Mr Franks and Mr Swanson get out and chat together leaning against the boot.

They waved at another car parking, and Miss Zaborowski, The Chaplain and Miss Haversham joined them, carrying robes over their arms.

Finally, a black Mercedes 8 series glided into the carpark, and Mr Winchester got out accompanied by Miss Pearl, Miss Lavender and

Miss Proctor, laughing like three mistresses. I looked through the binoculars at their feet and recognised the shoes I had seen in the woods. It was definitely them.

Sarah jabbed me on the shoulder with her finger, holding her phone trained on them, and pointing at my pocket. I dropped my binoculars around my neck and quickly took out my phone. I pinched the screen outwards with my thumb and forefinger to zoom in on their faces one-by-one, but Mr Franks and Mr Thornton were a blur as they left the group and headed for the pen.

I tried to follow them with my camera, but the zoom was too tight and all I could film was grass and branches until I widened the angle shakily. I couldn't hold still when I saw Mr Franks pull out his gun and walk towards a piglet, which squealed and tried to run away, but Mr Thornton held his arms out and they cornered it in the pen.

I couldn't watch when Mr Franks raised the gun, and closed my eyes, as a loud shot reverberated through the air.

I looked at Mason and his hand was perfectly steady on his phone, but Sarah had a tear in her eye and she dropped the phone to her waist as if it was too heavy to hold up.

They changed into their robes and Mr Franks lifted the piglet onto Mr Thornton's shoulders and he gripped it by the legs on his chest. It was exactly how Patrick had described it, except it was a piglet, not a lamb, but watching it happen with my own eyes was totally different. I could almost feel the pain of the piglet, and now understood how Patrick felt and why he needed to do something.

The others had changed into their robes with swords when Mr Franks and Mr Thornton returned and they all clapped, as if celebrating the murder of a defenceless piglet, before forming a procession in pairs into the woods. Half holding lit torches in the air and one swinging a brass bowl on chains from which the pungent smoke of incense was wafting in our direction.

I put my phone into my jacket pocket, 'come on, they're leaving.'

Mason got up but Sarah didn't move, 'I'm not going.'

'What's wrong, Sarah, are you OK?' I gently held her arm.

'We haven't got time for this,' Mason said, 'we'll lose them if we don't go *now*.'

'I'll be fine, I'll meet you back at the room. Go with Mason, quick.'

There wasn't time to argue and crouching low through the undergrowth I followed the direction the procession was heading in, being sure to maintain a safe distance, with Mason struggling to keep up behind me.

I watched them reach the clearing, the ceremonial bonfire in the middle which had already been prepared with a cone of sticks rising above logs, and Mr Thornton crouched and lowered the piglet onto the logs from his back. He lit a rag and suddenly the fire was aflame. I focused my phone on their faces, the flames casting flickering orange shadows on lips and chins, their eyes hidden behind the headdresses. I followed down their robes, passed their swords, to video their shoes.

They held hands and began to chant and walk around the fire in a circle.

'What are they saying?' I whispered to Mason.

'I don't know,' he said, 'it's not Latin, that's for sure.'

They stopped and then like doing the hokey-cokey ran towards the fire, still holding hands, and spat on it, before rushing back out, and then in again, three times.

They let go of their hands and held them out with their elbows bent in right angles, and palms open and raised their eyes to the stars and chanted. And then one of them walked to the fire and brought their hands together in prayer to their forehead, bowed to the pig from the waist, kneeled down and pulled out a piece of paper, scrunched it up into a ball and threw it on the fire, chanting, before returning to their place in the circle.

The one to their right did the same thing, throwing a scrunched-up ball, and returning until they all had done the same thing.

They chanted some more and then half of them suddenly pulled out their curved sickle swords and raised them in the air. I got a close-up of one sword glinting in the firelight and tracked down to their shoes. It was a man.

I picked up my binoculars and scanned the shoes of the people with swords as they chanted; they were all men, chanting in a deep baritone.

I looked at the others, alternately between each man, and noticed they weren't wearing ropes or swords around their waists and by their lips, the outline of their bodies and shoes, they were all women, which they began to kick off, standing in their bare feet in the dirt.

They pulled their arms in the sleeves of their robes and I saw their shoulders and bodies wiggle and fabric dropped around their ankles from below their robes, and they stepped out of them. They lifted the hem of their robes to their waist, revealing bare buttocks from the ones in front of us, and birds' nests of public hair from the ones opposite, and pulled the robes over their heads standing naked with their bare backs and breasts standing out.

I felt my face turning red and put my phone down, but like a dear trapped in headlights, I couldn't look away, as they proceeded to skip like a chain and weave themselves singing between the men with their swords raised. Even Miss Haversham!

Mason lifted his eyepatch and his eyes were so wide open it was like they were exploding, but he held his camera steady in both hands.

'We've seen enough,' I whispered, 'let's go. Mason? Mason? Let's go.'

'Hilary is so beautiful,' he said in awe, 'I never realised it.'

'Come on, Sarah said leave as soon as we get the evidence.'

'But *look* at her.'

'She's old enough to be your mother! Come on, let's go.'

'Can't we stay just a little longer, please Alex?'

'No! I'm going, you stay if you want. Can't you see their swords?'

We turned away and crept as quietly away as possible, and this time, I took extra care not to step on any branches. Gradually the singing diminished in the distance as we made our way back through the woods.

I couldn't get the picture of Hilary dancing so happy and carefree in her birthday suit out of my head, either, but cringed at the picture of Miss Haversham with her grey hair hanging down, swinging breasts like sacks, rolls of fat around her belly and heavy thighs. She was like a naked grandma! I had seen my baby sister having her nappy changed, but I didn't realise women were so hairy down there.

When we finally made it back to our dorm room, Sarah was waiting outside, sitting down against the wall, and we let her in.

'Did you see anything?' She said.

I looked at Mason and he looked down guiltily, and I did, too. It seemed much worse describing it to a girl, as if we were perverts or something.

'It was like watching a Roman orgy,' Mason said.

'You mean they were having ...'

'No! They were just naked,' I said.

'NAKED?' Sarah said, 'Mr Swanson? The girls are not going to believe this.'

'No! The women.'

'That's sexist!' she said.

'Who'd want to see a bunch of naked men prancing around.' Mason said.

'I'm curious, like every girl, there's nothing wrong with that. I bet you enjoyed ogling the women.'

'Are you joking, Miss Haversham?' I scrunched my eyes shut at the painful picture.

'Have you got it on video?' she asked.

Mason handed her his phone.

'O.M.G,' Sarah said watching them frolic, 'if you didn't have this, I wouldn't believe you. *Nobody* would believe you.'

'So, what do we now?' I said.

'First thing in the morning we go to the Police and tell them everything,' she said, 'Patrick's waiting.'

'Do we have to mention, Hilary?' Mason said, 'she's a very good counsellor. She might lose her job.'

'It's a bit late for that now,' Sarah said.

'Are you alright, Sarah?' I said.

She nodded but she looked very tired. More tired than us. This adventure had taken everything out of us all.

'Come here,' I said, and hugged her, 'You were fantastic, you know. You're a natural born leader.'

'You're the strong one.'

'What about me?' Mason said, feeling left out.

'Come here, Buddha boy,' I said, 'group hug.'

And we all hugged together.

CHAPTER THIRTY-NINE

Reporting to the police

In the morning, we all went to the House Mistress instead of going to registration, and told her we had information leading to the whereabouts of Patrick Mackensie, but we could only tell the Police directly. Mason had said we couldn't trust telling a teacher, because the teachers were involved, and Sarah and I agreed.

The House Matron drove us to the Police Station and in the privacy of the interview room, we told the Policewoman we had found Patrick Mackensie. She didn't believe us until she saw the photo of us with Patrick and checked the date of the picture on the phone. And then all hell broke loose.

She radioed in a code, and two plain-clothed detectives rushed in and asked us to repeat what we'd just told the Policewoman and examined the phone.

We were piled in the back of a Police car with blues and two's going, flashing lights and siren, all the way back to the school, where an ambulance was already waiting with its lights flashing.

We led the detectives, ambulance crew and caretaker, with a big bunch of keys, down to the lower ground floor in the North Wing, and the caretaker opened the door to the basement, undid the padlock and unwrapped the chain while the detectives shook their head at how we had got in, and finally opened the big Victorian gate.

They followed us between the mountain of coal and iron furnace and down the tunnel, opening the doors to the workers bedroom and toilet and scanning them with their torches until I put the light on for them.

We continued around the hidden dark bend at the end of the tunnel to the door with light streaming from below and knocked on the door.

The detectives suddenly pushed us aside, pulled out revolvers, I didn't even know they were carrying, shouted, 'POLICE! GET DOWN ON THE GROUND!' and kicked the door open.

'DON'T MOVE! KEEP YOUR HANDS IN THE AIR!' They shouted at Patrick Mackensie, while one threw the patchwork quilt off the bed, and looked under the bed, 'ALL CLEAR!'

The other one replaced his revolver, told Patrick to stand and put his arms out with his wrists together, and handcuffed him.

'Suspect identified and neutralised,' the detective called into his radio, 'ambulance crew ... What's your number?' He asked them and he repeated it down the radio, 'in attendance. I'll accompany him to the hospital and DC Bradford will interview three minors who are witnesses at the station with the S.L.O., DC White. Can you inform the family we found him.'

'Did you get the evidence?' Patrick asked us as the paramedic wrapped a blanket over his shoulders and led him out.

'You bet,' I said, 'it's all on camera. You did it Patrick. You beat them.'

'*We* beat them, Alex. The animals will be safe now. Whatever happens, that's all that matters. Remember that.'

'Come on, Patrick,' the paramedic said with his hand on his elbow, 'the ambulance is waiting.'

The detective ushered us out the room. 'You three are coming with me.'

'Does that mean we don't have to go back to lessons?' I asked.

The detective laughed even though I was being serious.

'You didn't find him,' Mason said, '*we* did. What about our reward?'

'There'll be plenty of time for you to ask questions at the station, after you've answered *mine*.'

When we were outside, the detective spoke to the headmaster, with Mr Winchester and Hilary standing beside him. She asked us if we wanted her to come with us to the station and Mason and I looked down guiltily, embarrassed to look her in the eyes, and shook our heads. We couldn't tell her she was in the video dancing naked that we were about to show the Police.

Mr Winchester smiled at us proudly, as if we didn't know about him, either. 'Well done,' he said to us, 'I'm sure your parents will be very proud. What's the matter, you don't look very happy. The detective said they couldn't have found you without him.' We couldn't exactly tell him he was in the video raising a sword to a burning piglet and spitting on it that we were just about to show the Police, either.

'We're still in shock, sir,' Mason said, and Sarah and I nodded rapidly.

'Of course,' he said, 'I'll let your parents know what a great service you've done to the community. You never know, I might even nominate you three for the headmaster's prize! What about that then?'

We smiled weakly.

The detective apologised but said we had to get back to the station. We all climbed in the back of the police car and were driven out the school front gate.

Sarah squeezed my hand, 'Don't worry, Alex, everything is going to be OK.'

I looked back out the window, and wondered if we'd ever see The Grange again.

CHAPTER FORTY

Taped interviews

A t the police station, this time we were all interviewed separately by the detective with DC White, the School's Liasson Officer from the school assembly, in attendance, so there was no point in lying about anything. They were also tape-recording it, which made me nervous.

I told them everything from learning about Patrick Mackensie's disappearance in the back of the House Matron's car to spying at the farm and showed them the video on my phone. I didn't expect them to confiscate it for forensic examination, but I had no choice. They brought me coke and packs of crisps but said they had no Maltesers.

They showed me an aerial map of the school with dotted lines indicating the boundaries of the school and asked me to pinpoint where the clearing was.

'Are you sure it's there?' The detective said, and then turned to the other one, 'it's on private land, outside the school boundary.' I wondered if that was why they didn't hold the ritual behind the farm.

They showed me a calendar and asked me to remember the times and dates when everything happened. That was the most difficult thing, and seemed to take forever, because I had to keep going back and changing days when they reminded me of things I'd said had happened.

I felt like I was the one in trouble and asked them if I was going to prison, like my father had, and they apologised and assured me I wasn't. I asked them about Sarah and Mason, too, and they said they weren't going to prison either, which was a big relief. But when I asked them about whether the teachers were going to prison, they said they couldn't discuss a current and ongoing investigation, which I suspected was a polite way of them saying yes. I felt bad about that, especially Hilary, who had saved me from suspension. I remembered Patrick saying saving the animals was all that mattered, but I had mixed feelings, and wondered if it had all been worth it.

'What about Patrick?' I said.

'It isn't illegal to run away,' the detective said, 'but it is never a good idea. He could have died down there and we would be none the wiser.'

'But they were murdering baby animals. He had to do something.'

'He should have come to us, that's our job.'

They didn't seem to appreciate, that the murderers were teachers including the Deputy Head, which to a kid, is exactly the same as the police, but it wasn't my place to argue with them.

Mason was sitting outside when I came out.

'I asked them about the reward,' Mason said, 'cash or cheque. What? We need to know these things. They said they didn't know because it wasn't coming from the police but Patrick Mackensie's father. So, I asked them whether they needed my bank details to give to his father. Don't worry, they know I meant business. I told them what we'd agreed in shares and I made sure they wrote it down. They said I was very prudent,' he finished with a proud smile.

'Where's Sarah?'

She stepped out of the ladies and her face looked white and drained but she smiled when she saw me.

'That was worse than the real thing,' she said, 'they never show this in the movies. We're all supposed to live happily ever after, not get the third degree from the police.'

'It didn't bother me,' Mason said, 'if they had done their job in the first place, we wouldn't be here. The police are fools, they don't even know Latin.'

Sarah and I were shocked when he said it, and then we all laughed.

PC White came out of the interview room and we all put on a serious face. 'We're finished here,' she said, 'I'll give you a lift back to school.'

We followed her out the back of the Police station where at least a dozen police cars were parked, I didn't know they had so many, and just as we were putting our seatbelts on, we saw a police van arrive.

Two policemen opened the rear door and held Mr Winchester's elbow as he placed his foot on the step—I recognised his shoes—his wrists in handcuffs, followed by Mr Thornton, Mr Franks, Mr Swanson and the school chaplain, all in handcuffs, too.

I tried to sink down in my seat so they wouldn't see me as we drove passed them, but I caught Mr Thornton's eye. He didn't look angry, like I thought he would, but helpless. Now he knew how the baby animals felt.

CHAPTER FORTY-ONE

Save the animals!

O n the last day of the Christmas term, the whole school and visiting dignitaries were assembled in the Grand Hall for the prize-giving ceremony.

I saw my parents sitting together at the back and waved at them over my shoulder. My father in his only three-piece suit smiled and my mother waved back.

The visiting dignitaries were sitting at the front in V.I.P. labelled seats alongside Mason, Sarah, Patrick and I in the front row, including the mayor, with a chain in a ribbon pattern tied by a medallion over his suit and tie, PC White and the District Police Chief in full uniform with colourful ribbons over his right breast pocket and Patrick Mackensie's father, the chocolate manufacturing King.

All the teachers, except for the conspicuous-by-their-absence omission of those involved in the ritual, were seated in black gowns along the back of the stage.

We all stood as the opening bars of the organ rang and sung the school hymn as the headmaster floated down the aisle in his mortarboard and black gown accompanied by the Head-boy and Head-girl, and climbed the steps at the side to take their seats on the stage in front of the staff.

The Grand Hall was silent as the headmaster got up and stepped to the podium.

'Ladies and Gentleman, The Grange Grammar School was founded in 1532 by Royal assent from King Henry the eighth and the school motto is, "Ex Spinis Uvas", grapes from thorns. I'd like you to think about that for a moment, because I'm sure you walk past it, muttering, 'What on earth is that?'

There were titters from the pupils at the funny expression he made like a schoolboy.

'We are first and foremost a Grammar school. That doesn't mean we only teach grammar.'

More laughs from the audience.

'We take pupils from every walk of life, some very rich and some very poor, but the one thing they all have in common, is ability: the *potential* to excel. We don't expect them to arrive perfect as the finished polished product. I certainly wasn't when I was twelve. Which is why our youngest pupils are like thorns, difficult to handle sometimes. I'm sure teachers and parents here will vouch for that.'

More laughs.

'However, in all seriousness, is that such a bad thing? To challenge, to question, look at things differently. Pupils constantly surprise me with their creativity and inventiveness and today's honourees are no exception. They truly represent the school values, what Grange Grammar stands for.

'Less we forget, the unicorn is a symbol of purity, innocence and power; the phoenix, a symbol of change and resurrection; The sword, a symbol of honour; And the scales, a symbol of fair play and justice.

'Like the unicorn, these pupils did not follow the accepted wisdom of their teachers and peers, but forged their own path. Like the Phoenix, they changed and adapted to all the obstacles in their path. Like the sword, they were forthright and honourable. And like the scales, their motivation was a sense of duty to the community for what they believed was right. These are the grapes, my friends, from the thorns.'

I felt a shiver down my spine, my palms were clammy and I dried them on my thighs. I looked at Sarah and she was blushing a beautiful crimson pink.

'This isn't the time or place to regale you with their adventures here, but it is extraordinary how they accomplished what they did and managed to maintain their grades and an otherwise outward semblance of normality. We owe an enormous debt of gratitude to them, and I think Mr Mackensie, you would like to say a few words on behalf of the family at this juncture.'

Mr Mackensie stood and climbed the stairs to the podium and shook the headmaster's hand as he returned to his seat. He took a deep breathe and pulled out a folded piece of paper.

'Firstly, I'd like to thank the headmaster for inviting us here today and his inspiring words. When my son, Patrick, went missing it was like our world collapsed.' His eyes became watery and he swallowed. 'I used to go to his bedroom, sit on his bed and hold his teddy bear,' he paused to regain composure, 'his room is full of stuffed toy animals, it was all we had of him.

'I prayed to God to find him and bring him home safe. Not knowing is the worst because you can't help imagining the worst. What if he'd been kidnapped or murdered, every possibility ran through our heads.

'Patrick's mother and I often went to sleep in tears, only to wake in the morning with the same pain and doubts. But I kept alive a small flame of hope in here,' he patted his heart, 'thanks to God. I would have given everything I owned to have Patrick back.

'I want to thank the police and in particular, PC White, for all their support and the incredible support we received from the school.' He turned back to the headmaster, away from the mic but we still heard, 'I mean that, thank you, Derek.' He turned back to the podium and pulled out three slips of paper from his inside pocket.

'Finally, I'd like to thank, from the bottom of my heart, the three pupils who found Patrick, and give them a small token of my appreciation.' He looked back at the headmaster who returned to the podium.

'Ladies and gentlemen,' the headmaster said, 'Alex, Sarah and Mason Armitage.'

I heard a huge cheer, thunderous applause, and pupils stamping their feet, as I stood nervously and climbed the steps to the stage followed by Sarah and Mason.

I looked out over the sea of smiling faces and I couldn't believe they were all clapping for us like we were heroes or something. I looked at Sarah and Mason embarrassedly as the entire Hall got to their feet, even the Mayor, PC White and the Chief of Police. Even Patrick Mackensie.

Mr Mackensie hugged me, slapped his arms on my back and handed me a cheque. I looked down and read the words, 'seventeen thousand five hundred pounds,' and my jaw dropped. I had to check the numbers in the box on the right and count the numerals after the comma, *thousands*. And it was real; it had his signature in blue ink in the bottom right-hand corner.

I stood aside as Sarah received her hug and cheque, and didn't even look at it, just waved her hand at the audience with a wide proud smile. It was so nice to see how happy and elated she was.

Mason was the next to be hugged and handed a cheque, and after quickly checking it, jumped up and down holding it up like the F.A. Cup, to more thunderous applause.

"Would you like to say a few words?' The headmaster asked us.

Mason stepped up to the podium and the headmaster bent the mic down for him, and people took their seats. 'Buddhism rocks. MEDITATE!' He shouted to cheers like he was a prophet or something, 'Oh, and thank you very much. Sarah?'

'Thank you to all my teachers for working so hard and teaching us to be INDEPENDENT WOMEN!' She hopped up and down as the girls screamed. I looked back at the teachers grinning, particularly the women.

'Alex?' The headmaster said, 'would you like to say anything?'

I swallowed as the applause died down and felt the weight of all the eyes on me in the Grand Hall.

'Thank you, Mr Mackensie, you don't know how much this money means to us. And I'd like to thank two very special people without whom I couldn't have got it.'

Mason and Sarah modestly lowered their chins to their chests.

'Firstly, my father. If it wasn't for him, I would never have come to this school. Thank you for believing in me, dad,' I saw my father wipe the corner of his eyes, 'and secondly,' Mason and Sarah looked up expectantly, I smiled at him in the front row, 'Patrick Mackensie ... SAVE THE ANIMALS!'

Patrick Mackensie jumped to his feet and cried out, 'SAVE THE ANIMALS!' All the pupils jumped to their feet and chanted, 'save the animals, save the animals,' except the Mayor and the Chief of Police who didn't seem to know why everyone was chanting and stared straight ahead politely clapping in their seats.

The headteacher took the podium and waited for the raucousness to die down. 'Funny you should mention that, Alex. I have one final announcement to make before we end with the school hymn.

'Some of you may have heard a rumour that the School Farm was being closed down. I have to say it was under review because it is non-profit making and runs at a significant cost to the school, which I explained to Mr Mackensie, and I understand Patrick would like to make a presentation. Would you like to join us on the stage, Patrick Mackensie?'

Patrick stood to wolf whistles and applause, his long hair tied back in a ponytail, looking younger and smaller in his school uniform than he did in the dungeon, as he climbed the steps. He hugged his father and his father handed him a cheque. Patrick shook the headmaster's hand and gave him the cheque.

The headmaster smiled and held up the cheque with two hands, 'one ... million ... pounds. The school farm will stay open!'

There were huge cheers and applause and the headmaster waited for the furore to die down before asking, 'Would you like to say anything, Patrick?'

Patrick shouted out, 'SAVE THE ANIMALS!' And punched the air with his fist.

'Save the animals, save the animals,' the chant rose again from the pupils. Patrick gripped my wrist and raised it in the air, and I grabbed Sarah's hand and raised it in the air, and Sarah grabbed Mason's hand and raised it in the air.

And for those few brief moments, we were all heroes, united, however long we lived.

The End

Epilogue

There was a note posted under our door when we came back from assembly. I opened it.

'Dear Alex and Mason

This is Hilary, I am writing to say I'm sorry, because we didn't get the chance to say goodbye properly, which is important to me.

Congratulations on your rewards! I would have loved to see you receiving them, but unfortunately, circumstances prevented me.

I know what you did, and I am proud of both of you, so never regret it.

I am a little bit embarrassed, to be honest, if you saw us in the woods. But never be ashamed of your bodies, or feel guilty, because we didn't choose them, they just happened to us; we're all the same underneath, in our souls, just the mechanics are different on the surface. Women don't understand theirs, any more than men, so never be afraid of asking questions. Our bodies are good.

Our minds are a problem, sometimes. But always remember, and I'm talking as a psychologist, we are what we think. If you feel upset, your feelings are always valid and that's the way of your thinking talking. We can always change what we think and feel better.

When parents argue, it doesn't mean they don't love you. We all think are parents are special, of course, but all they are, is grown-up kids, like me, like your teachers. We all do the best we can at the time.

The gathering was our way of making sure we did our best, although it must have looked strange to you. I doubt anyone's explained it to you, yet, so I'll try and keep it brief.

The sacrifice of swine is to ensure fertility, communication with the dead and the absolution of sin and dates back to the Bronze Age when pigs were considered impure.

We chant, 'he who gave these (offerings) to the gods – give (in return) to him at length, copiously, and widely!"

These words are from an ancient Assyrian rite called the tākultu ritual, and the sword the men carry is called the deified weapon, or Kakku, and is a symbol of the King, the men, who we call, amēlu gitmālu, a 'perfect man'.

We, the women, symbolise goddesses and we intercede on the Kings' behalf to the royal ancestors and then the gods.

At the return of the gods, the Kings give a prayer of raised hands, we call Šu'illa. We offer food and salt and burn incense to receive the Gods' blessing.

The notes we burn are a list of our sins so we can reach perfection and appease the Gods.

The women disrobe to be pure like the rivers and mountains, unadorned by material possessions, like Eve in the garden of Eden.

When I finish the ceremony, I feel lighter and free as a new-born baby, and all my fears, worries and stresses of the last month are washed away and I have the chance to be good again.

We never hurt the baby animals, and we never burned animals alive like the Police accused us of. They were always slaughtered humanely with a bullet to the head, and never in any pain, with the permission of the Farm Manager who sold them to us to help keep the farm going. And we never held the ceremony on school grounds, it was private land with permission from the owner.

The Police never charged us and nobody went to prison, you can always trust the Police. However, the Headmaster and School's Governing Body were not so generous and offered us the opportunity to resign rather than be dismissed for bringing the school's good name into disrepute. Appearances are everything in a school like this, as I'm sure you know.

In case you're wondering what happened to the teachers, we are all still friends.

Mr Winchester and Miss Haversham accepted early retirement, which they were planning to do anyway. Miss Pearl works for a homeless charity, Miss Lavendar runs a coffeeshop and Miss Zaborowksi is an actress in a travelling theatre company.

The chaplain is a full-time PhD student, Mr Franks has an online business, Mr Swanson is a personal trainer in a gym and

Mr Thornton works as an Antiquities tour guide in a London Museum. I have my own private practice. In a way, the change was a good a thing, in forced us to do what we always wanted to do.

Whatever you decide to do when you grow up, don't listen to anyone else, be true to yourselves. It's your life and you only get one. Although I can't help thinking, you'd make a fine psychologist one day, Alex, you have such a natural way with people, real empathy, insight and understanding, and you are a wonderful Buddhist, Mason, whatever you choose, there's a special place for you somewhere.

As we sing in the balağ, may the 'Lord, prince of heaven and earth,' and we answer in the eršemma, 'strong one, turn to me', bring you eternal light and happiness.

With all my love and best wishes,

Hilary.'

'What are you going to do with the money?' I asked Mason, folding the letter away.

'Put it in a bank, and let it work for me. My father said the bank pays you to just keep it there. It's like free money. What about you?'

'I'm going to spend half on a second-hand car for my father so he doesn't need to take the train and pay for a taxi to visit me. My mother told me not to give him money because he'd just spend it on drink and cigarettes. I'm going to buy my mother something special but I can't make my mind up.'

'You should ask Sarah; she'd know what women like. Did she tell you what she's doing with her money?'

'Yes, she wants to buy a horse. I know, what a waste of money. She's going to have to get up early every morning to muck it out in the school's stables, who'd want to do that? But she said it was her dream—shovelling horse's poop—I can't think of anything worse.'

Mason laughed, 'each to their own, I suppose.'

The door opened by itself and a voice said, 'Are you decent?'

'Speak of the devil,' I sighed, 'Come in, Sarah.'

She looked alarmed. 'You've got to come quickly. There's been an incident. This is important.'

A new adventure awaited, but that's a different story.

www.ingramcontent.com/pod-product-compliance
Lightning Source LLC
Chambersburg PA
CBHW050516260626
47157CB00004B/1346